MEN IN PERIL II

I0691417

First Edition

Published by The Nazca Plains Corporation
Las Vegas, Nevada
2010

ISBN: 978-1-61098-003-6
Ebook: 978-1-61098-004-3

Published by

The Nazca Plains Corporation ®
4640 Paradise Rd, Suite 141
Las Vegas NV 89109-8000

PUBLISHER'S NOTE
Men in Peril II is a work of fiction created wholly by *Christopher Trevor's* imagination. All characters are fictional and any resemblance to any persons living or deceased is purely by accident. No portion of this book reflects any real person or events.

Male Photo, Ekaterina Yudina
Art Director, Blake Stephens

DEDICATION

For Tony N. Trainer,

who does not even know the reason why.

MEN IN PERIL II

First Edition

Christopher Trevor

CONTENTS

INTRODUCTION

Greetings one and all and welcome to the second collection of stories of "Men in Peril." I was chatting online recently with my good buddy and ticklish star, the real-life Timmy Backman. I informed Timmy that when I start working on "Men in Peril 3", a tale of a battle of wills between him and a sexy female vixen that he wrote and submitted to me will be the lead story for that book. I am very happy to say that besides Timmy Backman's story of a man in peril I have other tales that my fellow authors have submitted to me. It would seem that "Men in Peril" has caught on and a lot of my author buddies are penning their most perilous ideas for just that, "Men in Peril." Besides authors writing about "Men in Peril" I have been very fortunate lately to also have met with some artists who draw "Men in Peril" very erotically and I must say that a lot these drawings are inspirations for upcoming tales. In the stories in this book there are no damsels in distress, just hunky, captured and worked over studly men. During our online chat Timmy said how just the words "Men in Peril" truly get him going and drive him crazy in a sexual sense. For Timmy who is a total submissive, a constant bondage and tickle victim and fetishist he is a man who truly defines a man in peril in the very erotic sense. For me personally I can recall as far back as when I was a young teenager and perhaps even earlier how seeing a man or men in peril was always so riveting for me. There is something about a manly man in peril that is truly intoxicating somehow for me. Its more entrancing than a woman in peril seeing as the man is supposedly always supposed to be the rescuer, the hero, the knight in shining armor so to speak. To see a man captured, bound up, held captive instead of the usual damsel in distress symbolically in a sense takes away that man's machismo. For me and for as long as I can recall most novels I have read have involved women in peril. I suppose this is why I appreciate books like "Messiah" by Boris Starling and "The Third Deadly Sin" by Lawrence Sanders, as both of these titles involved men being imperiled. All throughout the bible there are stories of men imperiled, of course the ultimate being Jesus Christ himself as he is tortured, made to carry his cross up a hill, beaten on the way and then finally crucified. The story of Jesus Christ's crucifixion had to be the most enthralling "Man in Peril" tale ever told.

But for me personally what started me on the road of enjoyment of seeing "Men In Peril" I would have to say was watching the old Batman, Superman and Wonder Woman TV series' when I was a young boy growing up. The death trap scenes in the Batman TV series were campy yet the bondage that Batman and especially Robin found themselves in, the positions they were splayed out in was intoxicatingly erotic somehow to my young mind. I never thought of it at that time in a sexual sense, but I do recall finding myself feeling very aroused for some reason at the bondage scenes depicted in Batman, so you can imagine how wonderful it was to find out about BDSM scenes when I started realizing I was Gay and a fetishist as well. The scenes of Jimmy Olsen, Superman's best pal always captured, tied up, and especially gagged in the old Superman TV series were as riveting to me as a captured Robin the boy wonder in Batman. What I found most intoxicating in those scenes were the way Jimmy Olsen always found himself gagged with a white cloth tied over his mouth. Most times of course Lois Lane was tied up by his side as well, as she and Jimmy Olsen always managed to get themselves into more trouble than any other newspaper reporters any of us have ever heard of. I often wondered as a young boy if being a newspaper reporter was really that dangerous and if reporters oftentimes found themselves kidnapped, tied up and placed in perilous situations.

When it came to the Wonder Woman TV series in the 1970s, for me it was all about the scenes wherein handsome soldier boy Major Steve Trevor constantly found himself captured, bound up, gagged and blindfolded. Like Jimmy Olsen, in Superman who was a reporter who always found himself imperiled I had to wonder if a lot of soldiers found themselves in the situations that Steve Trevor routinely did. When it came to Major Steve Trevor it was all a combination of the manly uniform he wore, his machismo and his rugged good looks as he struggled in bondage that really got me going. I suppose it can be said that Major Steve Trevor was a very large influence for me when it came to my military erotic stories that I have written and will continue to write.

Along with my own memories when it comes to "Men in Peril", like with the first collection of stories in this genre I asked some of my internet buddies to tell me of some of their early memories of what a "Man In Peril" meant to them. When did they first realize their attraction to a "Man in Peril?" Which characters riveted them hypnotically? Like with the first book I received some wonderful responses…

My buddy Adam, AKA Adam Nicks and the Poet Dreamer shares my attraction to Major Steve Trevor from the Wonder Woman TV series and comic books. Adam says that the handsome soldier boy was always getting either punched out or knocked out and then chained up or roped up. I could not agree more with that.

Another buddy of mine, this one named Bill, who enjoys the mixture of erotica, bondage and discipline says that for him Batman and Robin would be his first choice when it comes to "Men in Peril." Bill says, "Robin was always doing something he wasn't supposed to be doing and I really wanted to see Batman put him over his knee, pull down his tights and give him the spanking he really needed. The Flash and Green Lantern were others I would have liked to have seen with their superhero tights down and bare butts showing and being reddened."

My very good buddy, Tickle Master Vince offered a listing of handsome TV and movie actors who found themselves imperiled some of them in the most unusual of circumstances…

From Tickle Master Vince: "Here are a few of my favorite "Men in Peril" when I was growing up."

Larry Hagman in the 1965 TV series "I Dream of Jeannie" on an episode where his wrists were bound above his head and a whip was turned into a feather, and he was tickled silly.

Charlton Heston in the 1968 series of movies "Planet of the Apes", he was always barefoot, and the dominating apes could have tied him down and tickled his feet.

James Franciscus in the 1971 TV series "Long Street" he was a blind detective, and I always wanted him to be captured by some serial bad guy who might tie him up, remove his shoes and socks and tickle him senseless.

David Soul (of the 1975 series Starsky & Hutch) in the 1979 film "Salem's Lot" where he was strapped down and his bare feet were exposed.

Bill Bixby in the 1978 TV series "The Incredible Hulk", in any episode where his transformation would reconnect him back to his human form, he was always barefoot, and that seemed to make him vulnerable. Once he was no longer strong, he could easily be subdued and his feet could have been tickled.

My author buddy and good friend Ron Bossman offered these couple of paragraphs where his favorite "Men in Peril" scenes were concerned:

"As a child my favorite TV show was "The Big Valley." The show ran from 1965 through 1969. I had a huge crush on Lee Majors who starred in the show. The show depicted Lee in many different perilous situations every week. He often spent parts of the show shirtless, tied to a tree, or tied to stakes in the ground. I remember every episode very clearly. If the show didn't showcase Lee to my liking, well then, my imagination always took over. Later that evening in bed I would think of all the different things that I would have done to Lee if I was running the show. My imagination has always brought me many happy evenings."

"Much later in life as a college kid I can clearly remember a perilous situation of my own. A group of friends, all Gay, had gotten together one night for a game of Strip Poker. The game was going along as expected but a couple of us were getting close to having nothing on. One buddy came up with the great idea to add a little twist to the game. A naked guy could keep playing provided he agreed to do various tasks that the high winner of the round would choose. At this point the perils enter the scene. Remember, we were all around the ages of twenty to twenty one so we were all wild and horny all the time. Some of the tasks were simple. The winner would have the loser suck on his dick in front of us or perhaps lick his balls for a while. Unfortunately when I lost I got the winner with an imagination that equaled mine. I was tied to a bed and blindfolded with a guy's necktie. The rest of the guys took their time licking and sucking me. This went on for what seemed like forever. Then one of them got the bright idea to find out how ticklish I was. They somehow got their hands on a feather. I later found out that it was a feather from a Halloween costume with an Indian headdress. They really enjoyed hearing me howl with laughter. They quickly found my most sensitive spots and lingered there for quite a while. The rest of the guys had gotten tasks that lasted about ten to fifteen minutes. My task lasted about an hour. I got my revenge later in the game."

- Ron Bossman -

For my Leather buddy John Van Tuyl (who advanced his BDSM explorations with the help of dominatrices and under which more recently he composed "The BDSM-iad of John Van Tuyl- a long, largely autobiographical poem, whose annotations recall the same story) it was St. Isaac Jogues, SJ and the other "North American martyrs" who- still in their cassocks, were tied together and surrounded by a hot pack of near naked Iroquois! Thank you, Mom, for subscribing to the Catholic book club's condensed book series that included the story- and thank you, Iroquois and Jesuits alike, for fueling some of my first BDSM fantasies. You would think, after having referred to the book- well, at least, at the North American Martyr's chapter- so frequently in my youth (I must have seemed a model altar boy, taking it from the bookcase again and again- though no one knew that all my attention was riveted by only one of the four books that it presented in condensed form), that I would have gotten the volume-title more accurately when I sent this note.

- John Van Tuyl -

CRIMINAL BEHAVIOR (PART 1)

By Steve (and added onto by: Christopher Trevor)

Officer Rodney Graham had moved from the big city to a smaller, wealthy college town. The cop had undergone a shattering experience earlier in the year, and he thought that new surroundings, especially in a more peaceful location might help him overcome the trauma. He had refused to have any counseling- the officer was too ashamed by what had happened to him, and more importantly, by his reaction to the terrible indignities that he had been forced to suffer. He had been captured by a couple of criminals, been tied up, blindfolded and gagged, stripped of his uniform and sexually abused. Officer Graham was haunted by this experience. It was every cop's worst nightmare, to be captured and abused. Yet he could not get it out of his mind. Mentally, he reran the scene over and over in his head. What bothered him the most was the fact that he had become physically excited while he was bound and gagged and being abused. He had shot his load several times, once down the throat of another captive police officer. What was worse, he had been erect when forced to fellate one of the criminals, who had been wearing Rodney's own uniform, his uniform, which had been stripped off him.

The department had managed to cover up the kidnapping and sexual abuse of the two police officers. Rodney had the feeling that somehow Officer Patrick Curran's new friend Reggie had been instrumental in suppressing some damning evidence that would have destroyed the two police officers careers, but he wasn't sure how this had happened. Patrick seemed to have sprung back from the ordeal in a very short period of time; in fact Rodney could not remember seeing his fellow officer happier. Rodney could not even talk to Patrick about what had happened, or the aftermath. Rodney found himself standing in front of the mirror in his uniform, staring at himself as he relived the events of that night. He fought the temptation to take out his handcuffs and use them on himself, and to gag his mouth. But just thinking about it would cause his cock to harden. He couldn't stand it- he thought that if he moved he would be able to forget it and get on with his life.

Rodney threw himself into his new job, taking any overtime that he could, trying to immerse himself in work that he would be too tired and preoccupied from to think about his humiliating bondage experience. Williamstown seemed to be a quiet, low crime town- famous for its college and the adjacent art gallery. Little did the officer know that a major crime was being planned, and that he was going to play an important part in it.

The art gallery in Williamstown was crammed with treasures. A gang of art thieves had targeted the gallery and they had decided that they needed a diversion. They needed something that would have the town's police department distracted. After some deliberation they worked out a sinister plan. They would kidnap one of the local police officers, and a few hours later they would hit the gallery. The gang was hoping that the police would be concentrating their efforts on finding the missing officer, giving them a window of opportunity to snatch some of the best items from the gallery before there would be any effective response. They managed to stage a number of false alarms in the charming Victorian shopping area, hoping to lull the cops into a state of complacency. Then, they would kidnap one of the police officers, inform the police department of the kidnapping, and hit the gallery a couple of hours later. As part of their plan, they had managed to get a couple of the gang members' jobs in one of the businesses downtown. This was the spot where they would capture their cop.

Officer Graham prepared for the evening shift. He looked at himself in the mirror, almost against his will, admiring his uniform. Even though it was a different uniform from the one that he had worn in his previous job, he still felt the swelling in his groin. He tried to banish those thoughts from his mind. He adjusted his dark gray tie, which contrasted with the lighter gray of his shirt. The color of the tie matched the pocket flaps of his shirt. His trousers were also dark gray, with a red stripe running down the legs. He pulled on his black leather jacket, donned his hat and he was ready. With most of the students and much of the faculty out of town for the holidays, the town was much quieter than usual. The stores stayed open late, but by now most of them were closed. It would be another routine night. Officer Graham just hoped that he wouldn't have too many of the false alarms that had been plaguing the business area lately.

Tom and Hank were getting ready for the kidnapping. They had become such valued employees that Dan, the owner of the business, had entrusted them with closing up. Little did Dan know that the two so-called trusted employees had been responsible for the numerous false alarms that had been called in during the past few weeks. Everything seemed to be ready- they knew what time the cop on this shift usually patrolled the area. They would leave the back door of the premises ajar, just enough to lure the unwitting cop into the store.

Rodney drove through the quiet streets. So far there wasn't much happening. He had not even spotted any drivers who might be under the influence. The town was small enough that most people had the sense to walk to parties. He could see through the windows of some of the big old houses- people making merry, Christmas trees all lit up. Rodney felt a pang of loneliness; he hadn't made any new friends in town, and he had volunteered for duty on Christmas Day. He sighed, and turned onto Main Street. Hmm, that was odd. He could see a light shining from the office of Dan Vaughan's store. Dan was one of the few people that Rodney had become semi-friendly with since he moved there. He had bought some lures there for his Dad's Christmas present, and in fact had been in there earlier in the day, doing a little last minute shopping. He remembered that Dan had been groaning about having to attend a party that one of the professors at the college was giving that night. What was he doing in the store so late? Rodney decided to investigate.

Hank saw headlights shining through the window. He peered through the partly closed blinds. Show time! He saw the police cruiser slow down, and then stop outside the store. Their cop had arrived. Hank dashed to the storage area at the back of the store. It would take both himself and Tom to carry this out properly. Tom was probably sweating bullets right now; he had lost confidence after their last job- one reason why they had branched out. This was going to be a bit different from stripping houses of their contents.

Rodney climbed out of the cruiser, turned on his flashlight and shone it through the windows of the store. Nothing seemed to be amiss, but it wouldn't hurt to investigate. He thought about calling in, but decided that it would be premature to do so. Vera, the dispatcher was one tough cookie, and he had been exposed to her sarcasm more than once. Things were different here in Williamstown. However, it wouldn't hurt to check out the back door. Rodney walked down the narrow alley to the lane behind the store. He flashed his light over the brick wall. The back door didn't look quite right; it wasn't properly closed. The officer's hackles rose. Okay, he would just push the door open a bit he figured, and if anything looked out of place then he would call it in. The merchants in the area had been warned time and again about setting their alarms properly; if anyone had forced the door then the alarm would have gone off. Rodney gingerly pushed open the door, flashing his light into the darkness.

Hank and Tom waited, one on each side of the door. They could hear footsteps on the pavement in the alley behind the store and they saw the faint gleam of light. As the door opened the light grew brighter. Hank held a large fishing net in his hands. With his superior height, the plan was for him to throw the net over the cop, and then both he and Tom would tackle the officer. The door was now completely open, and the police officer stepped inside the storage room. Now was the time to act! Hank threw the net over the cop, and at the same time, Tom hit the light switch. Their prey had walked right into the trap!

Rodney flashed his light around the room. Everything seemed to be okay… suddenly something fell over his head. He dropped his flashlight as he found himself enmeshed in some kind of net. The officer tried to draw his gun, but found that he was helpless as he became tangled up in the mesh of the net. He dropped his flashlight and found himself almost blinded as the overhead light came on.

"What???" he bellowed but before he could get another word out he was knocked to the floor.

Two people jumped on him as he struggled, futilely thrashing around, trapped by the net that covered his body. He tried to get up, but the weight of his two assailants kept him trapped.

"Get his gun, get his gun!" the cop heard one of the men saying.

Rodney felt a hand thrust underneath the net, pulling his gun from his holster. He tried to get one arm free, but he was so tangled in the net that he couldn't move.

"Now the cuffs!" came the voice again.

"No, stop…" Rodney began but his head was banged against the floor as he tried to yell for help.

Stars floated in front of his eyes from the pain. As the net was removed he felt his arms being grabbed and twisted behind his back, hands fumbling with his gun belt, removing his handcuffs. Once again he tried to call out for help, but a hand went over his mouth, and another grabbed his nuts and squeezed tightly. He screamed through the hand gag, almost fainting from the agony. He was pulled to his feet, a hand still over his mouth and one grasping his groin. When he tried to struggle his arms were jerked up higher and the hand on his balls tightened its grip. The cop decided that he had to cooperate; he couldn't stand anymore of the arm cranking or the ball grabbing.

Hank listened to the cop sobbing in pain. Shit, Tom was getting carried away. Once the cop was cuffed he would take care of Tom. Ever since that last job that nearly got bungled, Tom had been suffering from a lack of confidence; but turning his anger on this helpless guy wasn't going to help him. Hank fastened the cop's hands behind him with his own handcuffs. Then he pushed Tom aside. The cop was gasping with pain, drawing in deep gulps of air. Hank knew that they had to gag him before he came completely to his senses. He yanked off the cop's dark gray tie and started rolling it up into a ball. He grabbed the cop by his light brown hair, and yanked his head up. He was startled by the luminous blue of the cop's eyes, even though they were swollen with tears of pain. Hank stared into those eyes for a moment and then shook his head. Had to keep the guy quiet.

Rodney gasped with relief when the tight hand grabbing his crotch was removed. He felt the cold steel of cuffs going around his wrists, his own damned cuffs no less, but he remembered the extra keys that he had taped to the band of his underwear. If these thieves, for what else could they be, just left him cuffed here, he would be able to reach the keys and free himself. Even as he thought this a hand gripped his hair and jerked his head up. The cop found himself staring into a pair of green eyes, surrounded by a black ski mask. He sucked air into his lungs, preparing to use the negotiating skills that he had been taught to use in this kind of situation. Before he was able to speak though, the man holding his hair ripped off his necktie and rolled it into a ball. The balled up tie was quickly shoved into the cop's mouth. Rodney choked on the cloth, trying to spit it out, but before he could do so, a piece of duct tape was pressed over his lips. He coughed and sputtered, but then another piece of tape went over the first. He howled miserably through the gag, as he watched his captor rip off another piece of tape. How much tape did they need to use to gag him? Then, he realized that this piece of tape wasn't meant for a gag. Everything went dark as he was blindfolded with the tape.

Hank looked down on the captive cop, sprawled on the floor of the storage room. Their captive seemed to be getting feistier, now that Tom's grip had been removed from his groin. They would have to package him up a bit better for transport. Tom opened his mouth to say something, and Hank hissed "SHHHH" at him. The quieter they kept, the better things would be. The criminal pair were working under false identities, and since they had clean records their fingerprints weren't on file, but the fewer people who knew that they were involved in this heist, the better it would be for them. Hank remembered waiting on this cop last week; if he didn't hear his voice there would be less chance of him identifying them. Officer Graham was starting to come to; they had better immobilize him now Hank thought. Hank quickly took rope out of the duffel bag. Time to tie this cop up really tight!

Rodney pulled at the handcuffs restraining his arms behind his back. He tried not to choke on the necktie that had been meanly stuffed in his mouth. His tape blindfold complicated matters. He was sure that if he was able to reach his spare keys he could free himself. All he had to do was wait for these two goons to leave. As he thought this he felt his ankles being grabbed. Shit, no, this was just going to make it harder to get free, but still, if they just bound his feet... His optimism evaporated in a very short period. His ankles were bound together, and then his knees. Okay, he could handle that, but then his legs were pulled up towards the small of his back...the bastards were going to hogtie him!

Tom and Hank, working in tandem, trussed up the helpless cop's feet and knees. The white nylon rope seemed to shine against Officer Graham's dark gray uniform trousers. The criminal duo pulled the rope as tightly as they could- they didn't want the cop kicking up a fuss when they carried him off. They had to make sure that the cop was completely restrained before they moved him from the premises. Hank could not believe it; he was usually prepared for anything! He cast his eyes around the storage room. AHA! That would work, he thought as his eyes lit on an extension cord that was hanging looped on the wall. It might be crude, but it would certainly be effective, at least in the short term.

Rodney grunted and struggled as he was hogtied. The cop knew that his chances of escape would be considerably lessened if he were hogtied. He tried kicking out with his bound legs, rolling around on the floor, trying to get away from the two men who were binding him, but it was useless. Handcuffed, gagged and blindfolded, he was no match for his captors. His nightmares, or his dreams, were coming true! He was tied up and gagged once again, and this time he could not pass off his sexual excitement as being a result of criminals handling his cock. He had hoped that was what had initially caused his erection the first time he was captured, but now he was rock hard, his cock pressed against the hard concrete of the storage room floor, dribbling pre cum into his boxers. And they hadn't even touched him down there, except for the first savage assault on his gonads. It wasn't until they had tied him up, gagged and blindfolded him, that he had become physically aroused. He rocked back and forth in his hogtie, trying to rub his erection against the floor. Somehow, the cop was turned on by his situation, helpless though he was, bound and gagged with his own gear. He felt the saliva in his mouth being soaked up by his necktie/gag, sealed in by tape. And it was his own cuffs that were holding his hands behind his back. The officer's mind was flooded by conflicting emotions. Here he was tied up, and possibly at risk of losing his life, and he was erect!

"Whew," Hank muttered, as he wiped the sweat from his brow. "Feisty bugger, isn't he? He sure as hell didn't want to get hogtied, did he? The bugger nearly broke my kneecap. But that should keep him quiet for a bit."

Rodney heard the two men muttering, and then their footsteps on the concrete floor, then silence. Had they gone and left him alone? He frantically renewed his struggles to free himself. If he could just reach the spare keys to his handcuffs…but his efforts to free himself were useless it seemed. No matter how much he strained, he couldn't get his cuffed hands even close to the hidden keys. The cop's muscles were screaming as he contorted his body, trying to reach his keys, or at least the knots in whatever it was that was hogtying him. It didn't feel like rope; it was something rubbery. His fingers could just about brush his bonds, but he couldn't reach the knots. Rodney felt sweat breaking out all over his body, soaking into his tee shirt. And all the time he fought against his bondage…he still had an erection!

CRIMINAL BEHAVIOR (PART 2)

By Steve (and added onto by: Christopher Trevor)

Hank pulled his partner out into the main part of the store.

"Tom, I'm going to dump that patrol car," Hank began. "If it stays out there too long, people will get suspicious, and we're not ready to let the cops know that we have one of their guys. We don't want anyone to start investigating too soon. Then I'll pick up your car. You keep watch over the cop, and NO fooling around, okay?"

"Yeah, sure Hank," Tom responded. "Get going and be careful."

Hank slipped out the back door into the deserted alley. As soon as he was gone, Tom turned his attention to their captive. Hank had to be kidding. Tom had been stuck in this hick town for the past six months, deprived of all things that he had held dear- fine clothing, fine dining and…other things. Hank had insisted that they keep a 'low profile', and do nothing that would call attention to themselves. Tom was in desperate need of some recreation, and he had this helpless cop lying here, unable to defend himself.

Tom looked down at the hogtied officer of the law. Damn, he was hot. Tom had noticed him around town before this; Williamstown being a small community. He was about five feet nine inches tall, stocky with light brown hair and killer blue eyes. This cop was just what Tom liked. He had always had a thing for men in uniform, and who knew when the chance would come his way again? The cop was lying on his stomach, not moving or making a sound. Tom thought that he had better check him out, just to make sure that he was still breathing. Hank couldn't object to that could he?

Tom rolled the captive cop onto his side. Mmmm, he was looking good. His light gray uniform shirt had been pulled open at the collar when Hank had ripped off his necktie to use as a mouth stuffing. The cop's white tee shirt showed through the open collar. Mmm. Tom's fingers started tingling. Should he open the shirt and the leather jacket a bit more to see what was inside, or…go for the big time right away? It wouldn't hurt to check both of them out- Tom had to make sure the guy was still alive, didn't he? The cop still wasn't making any noise, just lying there like a lump on a log. Further investigation was required.

Rodney held himself quiet as he was rolled on his side. This was it then, what every cop dreaded. He waited for the foot in the gut, the bullet piercing his skull, the knife slashing his throat. Instead, he felt hands pulling his shirt open, rubbing his chest through his shirt. NO! He wasn't going to let this happen to him again, at least not without a fight. He had to prove to himself that he wasn't some kind of pervert. Even as he thought this, his cock, which had shriveled up when the intruders had walked into the storage room, sprang to life. NO!!! This wasn't happening to him. He was normal, he was a normal cop! He screamed defiantly through his tie stuffed mouth, and began struggling frantically against his bonds, forcing his aching muscles to fight. With a huge effort he flipped himself away from the marauding hands. With all his might, ignoring the terrible pain in his shoulders and thighs, he pulled at the cord that bound his hands to his feet. If only he could reach his spare keys, the cop would be able to defend himself.

"Whoa, I've got a live one here! Guess I don't have to check any vital signs to see if this cop is still alive," Tom chortled to himself, not thinking to keep his voice down.

Damn, this was going to be fun. He always enjoyed it when they put up a fight, and the fact that his victim was a cop just doubled his anticipated pleasure. Having a man is uniform, tied up and gagged, screaming and kicking made his cock harden immediately. Lucky for him that this was the cop on duty, not fat old Harry Watkins. This was a cop and cute to boot. Too bad those blue eyes were all covered up by duct tape. Tom would have liked to see them bulge in fear. This cop reminded Tom of some of the frat boys who had made his life a misery when in college. A cop and a frat boy combined! Oh yeah, he hoped that Hank took a long, long time coming back. He was ready for some long overdue rest and relaxation.

Tom rolled Rodney back onto his side, and pinned him down with his hand.

"Going somewhere big guy?" Tom teased the captured cop. "I don't think so. You see, I'm going to have some fun with a hot cop, and there's nothing you can do about it."

He slid his hand back inside the cop's uniform shirt, finding a nipple and massaging it through the fabric of the sweaty tee shirt. Interestingly enough, the nipple sprang to life under his manipulative fingers. The cop was still trying to rock back and forth, he was yelling through his gagged mouth. Gee, he had a lot of life in him Tom mused. Tom could see the sweat breaking out on the cop's forehead, over the strip of duct tape that blindfolded him. His head was twisting back and forth, and it was obvious that he was trying to get rid of the necktie that was stuffed into his mouth and sealed in with tape. Good thing that they had used two long pieces of tape to gag him. It wouldn't be convenient for him to be alerting any passer-by. Tom started rubbing himself as he listened to the muffled cries. He hooked a leg over the cop, further holding him down. He needed both of his hands free now. The time to bring himself off would come later. First he had to get his captive primed and ready.

Rodney felt tears of humiliation come to his eyes as hands rubbed his chest, causing his nipples to spring to life. He tugged on his cuffs and the ropes and cord that bound him. The metal cuffs dug into his wrists as he struggled. He thought that he detected a slight loosening of the cord that kept him hogtied. If only he could get free of the hogtie, he would have a fighting chance. He tried in vain to get rid of the necktie, now thoroughly soaked with his saliva, drying up his mouth, but the double pieces of tape that held it in refused to budge. Rodney felt himself burning with shame as the molestation of his body continued. He was normal, he kept on telling himself, he was normal! Please God, don't let him go any further!

Tom had the hapless cop pinned down and continued to rub his hands over the cop's chest, playing with his nipples, getting them hard, every now and then giving the nips a squeeze. The way the officer squirmed under him, muttering curses through his gagged mouth was making Tom harder and harder. He had a lot of pent-up energy to expend. It had been six months since he had any fun, and the preppy neighbor of his last burglary victim hadn't been nearly as hot as this frat boy cop. Tom leaned over and smelled Rodney's leather jacket. Oh yeah, this was good. The cop was fighting him off as best he could, hogtied the way he was, but he didn't seem to be making much progress. Tom gave a final squeeze to the cop's nips and pulled his hands out of the uniform shirt. He licked his lips as he prepared to investigate the lower regions of Rodney's body.

Rodney gave one final tug to the electrical cord that bound his hands to his feet, and felt one of the knots give way. Panic had given him renewed energy. When his captor removed his hands from inside his shirt, he was sure where they were going to go next. No way was he going to let this guy find out what was inside his trousers, to have his shame exposed. He heaved his body up, catching the guy who was straddling him by surprise, knocking him over. The cop heard a muffled exclamation, and then a loud thump. Then…silence. Rodney worked feverishly. His shirt had already been pulled out of his trousers during his struggles. Now all he had to do was to get the spare keys to his handcuffs and he would be free. He got his fingers inside the waistband of his underwear. Yes, there they were, taped in place. He fumbled with the tape, unpeeling it carefully. YES! He had the keys between his fingers. It would only take him a moment to unlock the cuffs. Damn, he had dropped them on the floor! He searched desperately, his fingers squiggling around crazily, groping. The trapped officer's task was made more difficult by the fact that his hands were cuffed behind him. YES, there they were again. He had them in his grasp. Now, he needed just a minute more…this would be so much easier if he wasn't blindfolded the cop thought miserably. He could hear the man he had knocked off him starting to groan. Rodney's hands were so slippery with nervous sweat that his task was now even more difficult than it should have been. There, the key was in, turning…

Hank swore to himself quietly. He had dumped Officer Graham's patrol car a couple of blocks from the store, and then made his way on foot to where the car that he had been provided for them had been dropped off. A stolen car, with fake plates, there was nothing that could connect it to the false identities that Tom and Hank had been living under. Just as he had left the sporting goods store, an intense snowstorm had begun. He could barely see as he drove the patrol car, his nerves on edge as he waited to be stopped. The thug had heaved a sigh of relief when he got rid of the cop car, but the drive back to the store in his own car had been treacherous. Now all they had to do was to load their captive into the car, and make their way to the designated hideout. Hank hated driving in the snow, but he knew that he would have to do it. Tom was an idiot when it came to winter driving. He carefully maneuvered the car into the alley behind the store and disembarked from the vehicle. He pushed open the back door of the store, and stopped dead in his tracks. Tom was lying prone on the floor, and the cop had his handcuffs undone. He was in the process of pulling off the strip of tape that had been used to blindfold him. Shit, what the hell had Tom been up to? That cop had been so securely bound, there was no way that he should have been able to get loose!

Rodney gave a sob of relief as he got one hand free. He ripped off the duct tape that blindfolded him, wincing as it pulled at his eyebrows and eyelashes. He had just removed the tape when the back door opened. For a moment he thought that help had arrived, but then he saw the man who entered pull a gun and aim it straight at him. Oh shit. Rodney started ripping at the tape that covered his mouth. He knew that he would not have time to undo the ropes around his ankles. Just possibly someone might hear him if he yelled for help. He yanked off the first piece of tape from his mouth, then the second. He spat out his soaked necktie, and tried to draw a deep breath.

Hank sprang into action. He rushed into the room and tried to jump onto the cop. But the cop rolled to one side and Hank landed on the concrete. The bugger was trying to crawl away from him, and he was starting to make some noise. Not much yet, only croaking sounds were coming from his mouth, but give him a minute and he would be making a racket, if he could. Hank had no intention of giving the cop the chance. The thug made another grab for the cop. His hand slid off the smooth leather of the cop's jacket. Damn, this guy was slippery as an eel, even with his feet tied. Still, he couldn't…FUCK! Hank fell back, clutching his face in pain. The bastard had swung out at him with his fist, and the loose bracelet of the handcuffs had caught him across the nose. Tears of pain came to his eyes. Oh God, this hurt. Through the haze of pain, he heard the cop start to yell for help.

Rodney had seen the hulking figure spring towards him, and instinctively he rolled to one side. He heard the big guy grunt as he landed on the concrete floor. Rodney began scooting backward, trying to untie his feet at the same time. Damn, his fingers wouldn't work; they were too stiff after his period of bondage. He attempted to yell for help, but his mouth and throat were still dried up from having had his tie stuffed in there. He moved his tongue around his mouth, trying to get the saliva flowing. Rodney threw himself to one side as the big guy lunged at him again. He felt the hands of his abductor slide over his jacket, just missing pinning him to the floor. Rodney swung his fist; his blow didn't strike the guy in the face as he intended, but he felt the empty cuff make contact, and heard a scream of pain. Rodney took a deep breath and yelled, "Help me someone…GGGGGMMMMMPPHHHHHH."

Tom had cracked his head on the floor when Rodney had pushed him over. He laid prone, in a daze, stars spinning in front of his eyes. He was vaguely aware of frantic movements next to him, and then he felt a gust of cold air as the door opened. As he came to his senses he realized that Hank had returned and was tussling with the cop. Good old Hank, always coming to the rescue. Wait a minute that was Hank yelling. What the hell… Tom pushed himself up as he saw Hank rearing back, clutching his face and yowling in pain. Crap. Then the cop started yelling. That wouldn't do at all. Tom launched himself at the cop, knocking the man in uniform flat on his back.

"Shut the fuck up Pig!" Tom rasped and pressed a forearm against the cop's throat and put a hand over his mouth.

As he felt the cop struggling under him, trying to yell through the hand gag, he felt himself getting hard again. It was going to be a real treat teaching this cop a lesson.

Rodney tried to fight off the man who had him pinned to the floor, but it was a fruitless battle. His muscles were still aching from the bondage and his struggle to get free. The blow that had disabled the big guy had been a fluke. He hoped that someone had heard his cry for help. The arm pressing down on his windpipe was cutting off his supply of air. He attempted to pry the arm off but with the other guy's body pressing down on him he didn't have a chance. Everything started to go dark.

CRIMINAL BEHAVIOR (PART 3)

By Steve (and added onto by: Christopher Trevor)

Hank staggered to his feet.

"I told you not to fool around with him, you asshole," Hank ranted at Tom. "Let's hope that no one heard the cop. Help me to get him ready to go. Its snowing like crazy out there, the roads are going to be hell."

"Hank, I just," Tom began.

"Shut-up you fool," Hank seethed, cutting Tom off. "Grab a couple of sleeping bags from the store. I'll get this boy ready for the trip."

He heard the cop start to groan. Time to gag that bastard again. Hank felt his nose. It wasn't broken, but it sure hurt a lot. It might be an idea to give the cop to Tom. It might make Tom calmer, and the blow to his nose had really ticked Hank off. The cop was going to pay for that, one way or the other. The cop's moans were getting louder. It really was time to shut him the fuck up. Where the hell had they put that duct tape? Hank found the cop's spit soaked tie lying on the floor. He knelt down next to the cop, and held the tie against his lips.

"Open up Piggy, time to eat your tie again," Hank chuckled mockingly.

The cop closed his mouth firmly and turned his head away. He could smell his own saliva on his uniform tie. Hank grabbed him by the hair and jerked on it, hard.

"I said, open up!" Hank seethed now. "Trying to be Mr. Tough guy? Well, how do you like this?"

Hank pulled harder on the captive cop's hair. The cop opened his mouth to cry out in pain, and Hank popped in the balled up tie. He shoved it in as far as it would go and heard the cop choking on his own neckwear. Hank laughed and felt a certain sense of satisfaction. Good. Hank's nose was throbbing, and he was in a vindictive mood. So long as the guy didn't choke to death, Hank was happy if he was uncomfortable. Damn, where was that tape? He would have to use something else. Hank could see that Tom had been busy; the cop's uniform shirt was open and his undershirt was pulled up, exposing his nipples. That would work. Hank got to work tearing the undershirt off the cop. The thin cotton fabric ripped easily. He tore off a long strip, made a big knot in the middle, and forced it between his captive's teeth. He tied it off at the back, pulling it as hard as he could. He wanted to make sure that the gag was tight and not easily removed. Yep, that should do the job. He tore another strip from the undershirt, and tied it around the cop's head, covering his eyes again.

Tom came back into the storage room, laden with a sleeping bag, and some other supplies.

"I've brought some bungee cords as well," he said.

Hank was about to reprimand his companion in crime when he realized that it was most likely too late to worry about disguising their voices. He had spoken as well. Too bad. With their share of the loot, they could relocate somewhere nice and warm. No more of these North-eastern winters. No one knew their true identities in any case, though if their pictures were broadcast; it would just be a matter of time before someone identified them.

Rodney sobbed miserably in frustration through his gag. Escape had seemed so close. He tugged on the cuffs that Tom had put back on him when he had passed out. The officer could not ignore his throbbing erection. He tried to will his cock to go down, but his body disobeyed his brain. NO NO NO. Why was he responding like this? For months he had been fighting against these strange desires. He did not want this to be happening to him, he really didn't. He was having flashbacks to his earlier humiliation in the city- being jacked off, forced to lick up cum, having cock shoved down his throat- and it just made him harder. No, I'm normal! This can't be happening to me! Then he felt rough hands on his body, rubbing his swollen crotch.

"So the piglet likes what's happening to him," the trapped cop heard hissed into his ear. "Who would have thought it?"

Something warm and soft was pulled over Rodney's head, and then over his shoulders, and further down until his entire body was enveloped. He fought valiantly, but he was helpless, totally vulnerable. The cop gasped for air as he realized that he was being stuffed headfirst into a sleeping bag. He bucked in panic, jerking his body frantically. He would suffocate! It was useless. Something tight was being wrapped around the sleeping bag, securing it in place around his body. Only his feet were sticking out of the end of the bag. Almost immediately sweat broke out on Rodney's body. It was so warm and stifling inside the sleeping bag.

The two criminals picked Rodney up, bundled into the sleeping bag, and headed out into the storm. It took just a minute to pop the helpless cop into the trunk of the car, and slam the lid down on him. It was time to get moving.

Hank and Tom hopped into the car, and set off into the snowstorm. Hank picked up his cell phone.

"Yeah, we've got him," Hank said into the cell phone. "There's been a hitch, but not to worry. The patrol car is in Dedham- I left his radio and badge on the front seat. Yeah, yeah, I know what to do. The snow might complicate things, but it should work out for us. Three hours? Okay, yeah, there had been a change of plans. Hey listen, don't worry, I know what the hell I'm doing. Yeah, good luck."

At that Hank clicked off the cell phone and looked over at Tom.

"Change of plans, Tom, my boy," Hank said. "We're going to be staying in town. We're heading back to the house. No one will connect us to this, at least not for a long time, and with all this snow there'll be less opportunity for us to get stuck."

Hank drove slowly and carefully through the snow-covered streets. He didn't want to get into an accident- it would be awkward, to say the least, in more than one way with a cop, tied up and stuffed in the trunk. Luckily, the house wasn't far away. So far, so good. No lights in the houses on either side- even better. With any luck, no one would notice them carrying the captive cop inside. He pulled up in front of the house. Tom and Hank got out of the car and Hank popped the lid on the trunk.

"You get the head, I'll take his feet," Hank ordered.

The two men grabbed the bagged up Rodney and carried him through the deepening snow to the side entrance of the house. Opening the door, they dumped him on the floor.

"Okay, what next, Hank?" Tom asked and Hank grinned.

"I saw that you had started something while I was away," Hank replied. "Why don't you finish it? I know that I said no fooling around, but we're stuck here, and…who's going to tell? I doubt the cop here will want to broadcast the news. Think what it would do to his reputation; he wouldn't last on the force for a week if word of this got out. Tommy, I think we have carte blanche, so long as we don't leave any permanent damage. You have your fun with the cop; I've got some loose ends to straighten up here."

Tom loosened the bungee cords that he had tied around the sleeping bag containing Rodney and pulled it off, uncovering his prize. The cop lay on the floor moaning, his uniform shirt pulled open, exposing his chest, his hands once more cuffed behind him, his feet tied together. Most of his face was obscured by the blindfold and gag made up of strips of his torn undershirt. Tom licked his lips. He was going to have some fun with this cop tonight. He could feel his cock harden as he thought about what he was going to do. He would teach this cop a lesson he wouldn't forget. He reached down and grabbed the cop by the collar of his leather jacket, pulling the officer upright. He started dragging the cop over to one of the kitchen chairs; he knew what he wanted to do first. He remembered how the cop's nipples had sprung to attention when he had been feeling up his chest. He had been rudely interrupted before he could investigate any lower. Now was the time. But first, he wanted to get the cop looking like he would if he were on duty. Just one little tweak to the nipples…yep…and the cop moaned through his gagged mouth as his nipples hardened. Hmm, it really looked as if the captured cop *was* enjoying this. But first he had to prepare him.

Rodney took in as much breath as he could when the sleeping bag was removed. He had nearly stifled inside that damned bag, sweat breaking out all over his body. What the hell was going on here??? He tried to collect his thoughts, but before he could do so he felt the collar of his leather jacket being grabbed and he was dragged across the floor. He tried to struggle, but he was exhausted and stiff from the bondage. The tight cuffs were cutting into his wrists and the rope around his ankles was still in place. He moaned through his gag as he was picked up and thrust into a chair, hands going inside his open shirt, rubbing his nipples. Oh shit, his cock was hard again, and so were his nipples. Then, hands were at the back of his head, untying the cloth that was wrapped around his eyes. He blinked in the light, trying to focus on his captor, but all that he could see was a figure clad in black from head to toe. The guy was bending down, pulling off one of his heavy boots. What the hell???

Tom removed one of his boots, and then pulled off his thick boot sock. He had to get the cop looking all nice and tidy again, and for that he would need the tie that was stuffed in his mouth. His sock would make a good replacement for the tie; too bad for the cop that he had been wearing this pair for a couple of days. He balled it up in his hand and leaned over the cop sitting in the chair.

"Smell that, piggy wiggy," Tom laughed as he waved his thick sock under Rodney's nose. "You're going to do more than smell it in a minute. You're going to be chewing on it. Nice and ripe isn't it?"

He pressed the rank sock over the cop's nose. Damn, but this guy was wriggling around like an eel. Tom would have to fix that before they went any further. Nimbly sidestepping the bound booted feet that were kicking out at him, he retrieved one of the bungee cords that he had used to tie around the sleeping bag. CRASH! The cop had managed to get off the chair and was crawling across the floor. Tom picked up the cord and walked over to the officer. He wasn't in a hurry, the cop wasn't going anywhere fast. Laughing meanly, Tom reached down and scooped his bound captive cop up in his arms. He quickly dumped him back in the chair, making sure that his arms were draped over the back of it. The thug straddled the cop, slowly zipping up the officer's shirt, staring into those luminous blue eyes that were pleading with him. The cop was shaking his head from side to side, mmmmphhhhing through his tie stuffed mouth, and still trying to get up out of the chair, but it was useless. Tom's weight kept Rodney pinned to the seat of the chair. There, that was done, the shirt was zipped up. Tom stood up and started wrapping one of the cords around the cop's waist, securely fixing him to the chair. He was going to have to do something about those feet though. He didn't want the cop kicking him, and in any case, he wanted those sexy cop legs spread wide.

Rodney had recoiled as his kidnapper had held the smelly sock over his nose. NO! There was no way that he was going to have that damned rancid sock stuffed into his mouth. Oh, but why was his cock jumping like this? He could feel it sticking through the fly of his boxers, rubbing against the fabric of his uniform trousers. He kicked at his captor, but failed to make eye contact. The guy walked away and Rodney took the opportunity to make an escape attempt. He heaved himself out of the chair and rose to his feet, but almost immediately fell to the floor. Though winded, he began crawling across the kitchen floor. The cop hadn't gone more than a few feet when he was picked up by strong arms, and shoved back into the chair. He tried to struggle, but his captor sat down in the chair, and began doing up his shirt. Rodney shivered as he felt fingers sliding inside his shirt as it was done up, brushing against his nipples, making them hard again. Then the guy got up and meanly bound him to the chair. Rodney kicked out at him once again, in a futile effort to disable his kidnapper. He missed, and the man in black knelt down on the floor and began untying his feet. One end of the long rope that had bound his feet was knotted around his left ankle. The man tying his feet got up and walked behind the chair, yanking Rodney's left foot as far back as it would go. Rodney grunted in pain, and then a hand was on his right foot, pulling it back, and the other end of the rope being knotted around his right ankle. Now his legs were spread wide, his bulging crotch visible and vulnerable. Tears of shame came to Rodney's eyes. There was no way that the guy who had bound him to the chair could miss the erection that was tenting Rodney's uniform trousers. As the cop jerked in his bondage he could feel the head of his cock being chafed by the rough cloth of his trousers. He looked down and could see a dark spot forming. Why was this happening to him?

Tom was ready to re-gag the cop. He loosened the knot of the strip of torn tee shirt that held the cop's tie inside his mouth. The cloth fell down around the officer's neck and Tom stuck his fingers inside Rodney's mouth. He extracted the saliva soaked tie. Rodney coughed and sputtered miserably as the cloth was removed from his craw.

"Let me go you freak, you're in big trou...MMMMPPPHHHHHHH..." was all Rodney could say and Tom laughed as he shoved his dirty smelly sock into the cop's mouth, pushing it deep into his throat.

He groped himself with his free hand as he listened to the cop choking on the rancid sock. Oh yeah, this was hot. Tom couldn't wait to start working on this guy. He pulled up the strip of cloth hanging around Rodney's neck, and pushed the fat knot between his teeth, holding in the soiled sock. He walked behind his cuffed captive and tied the cloth behind the back of his head, pulling as hard as he could on the ends as he knotted it. That looked really fucking hot, the cop's cheeks bulging over the strip of cloth, his blue eyes spitting fire. Tom was going to enjoy breaking this guy. He picked up the sodden tie from where he had dropped it and clipped it in place.

"There, you look almost the way you should," Tom taunted the captured cop. "Too bad you're missing your badge and radio, and that holster of yours is empty. Now for the finishing touch...look what I brought with me, Cop."

Tom pulled out Rodney's uniform hat, now slightly battered and placed it on the cop's head. The thug licked his lips. The cop looked so hot in his uniform, his hands cuffed behind him, tied to the chair, his mouth gagged, his legs spread wide open. Tom could hear the muffled curses coming from the cop's mouth. Well, he could curse as much as he liked; there wasn't anything that he could do to stop Tom.

Rodney choked on the taste of the dirty sock stuffed into his mouth. Christ, this guy must sweat like a pig Rodney thought; either that or he had been lying, and had been wearing his damned socks for a week. The strip of cloth securing the sock in his mouth was tied so tightly that he could feel his cheeks bulging over it. The knot in the middle of the cloth, between his teeth, was so large that there was no way that he would be able to spit out the sock. He tugged at the cuffs holding his hands behind his back. With his spare keys gone there was now no way that he would be able to get his hands free. The muscles in his thighs were aching, from the awkward position in which his legs were bound. His captor started walking towards him, rubbing his crotch as he approached. Oh God, what was going to happen to him the cop wondered. Rodney started struggling fiercely, rocking back and forth in the chair.

Good. The cop was fighting against his bondage. That would make it more fun. Gee, he looked and sounded pissed. Tom hunkered down in front of his captive.

"Hmm, and what do we have here Officer?" Tom teased the cop. "It sure looks like you've got something stuffed in your pants. I wonder what it could be. Surely a macho cop like you wouldn't have an erection. Not while you're all tied up and gagged with my dirty sock. But hey, let's take a look."

Tom pulled down the zipper of the grey uniform trousers and stuck his fingers inside. He extracted the erect cock, and it flicked with a finger.

"My, my, my, you seem to be oozing here Officer," Tom chuckled. "And you have been for quite some time, judging by all this crusty stuff on here. Now I wonder why you are so hard. I guess you like being tied up and gagged in your uniform. What do you have to say for yourself?"

Tom started jerking on the hard cop cock, listening to the officer yelling through his gag.

"MMMMMMMNNNNOOOO!" Rodney pleaded. "MMMMSSTTOP!!"

The cop was shaking his head back and forth, begging through his gag, jerking against the ropes that held him fast to the chair.

"You like this Cop?" Tom asked the trapped officer. "You want me to do some more? Sorry, I can't hear you. You'll have to speak up."

Rodney closed his eyes in shame. He could not believe that he was still erect, with this goddamned criminal handling his cock. Why did it feel so good? He bit down on the knotted cloth tied between his teeth. No, he wouldn't cum. He would be strong. He fought against the cuffs and the ropes tying him to the chair. With his legs spread there was no way that he could defend himself. He was helpless and totally defenseless. He could feel the sweat trickling down his face as he willed himself not to cum. As he struggled his uniform hat fell to the floor. The cop couldn't stand this much longer. This fucking guy has to stop, Rodney thought, or else...No, he wouldn't...oh shit..."

"UUUUUUHHHHH..." Rodney gasped through his stinking sock gag.

Tom quickened the pace. The cop was groaning, his face turning red as he squirmed in the chair. Inarticulate moans replaced the muffled curses. Tom grinned as his captive whimpered, now bouncing up and down in the chair, his eyes squeezed shut as his breathing became more labored.

"MMMMMPPPHHHH!!!" Rodney groaned.

It looked like the cop was getting closer to shooting his load, the way he was wriggling and moaning. Oh yeah, and here it came...

"Hey, it looks like Old Faithful down here, Officer," Tom joked. "You must have had juice stored up in there for a week. That was quite a load for a cop to shoot while he's all tied up and gagged. Gee, you really made a mess all over yourself, didn't you?"

Rodney looked down on himself, as he panted through his gag. He could see his own cum on his wrinkled and wet tie, on his shirt, running down his leather jacket. The cop could even feel stickiness on his cheeks. His captor continued playing with his cock, rubbing the sensitive head.

Tom laughed at the trussed up cop, who was staring at him, despair showing in his blue eyes. The thug scooped up some of the spooge that had landed on the cop's leather jacket and rubbed it in the officer's face, holding his sticky fingers under his captive's nose.

"How do you like the smell of your cum, Pig?" Tom asked the captured cop. "You had quite a load in there…I wonder how much more there is in those balls of yours. I'll just have to find out, won't I? But before we do that, I have needs of my own that have to be taken care of. You don't want to be selfish, and be the only one to cum. Just let me clean these messy hands of mine."

Tom wiped his hands in the captive cop's hair. Rodney was infuriated. Once Tom's hands were clean he started to unzip his fly.

Rodney's eyes widened in apprehension as he watched his captor pull down the zipper of his jeans and put his hands inside the fly. The guy grunted as pulled his dick out of his underwear. It was hard and dripping. Rodney shrank back in the chair as the man approached him, cock in hand. The cop strained against his bonds, even though he knew that he could not get loose from the handcuffs. If only he could free his feet, he might be able to fend this guy off, or at least inflict some damage on him. But the ropes held fast. Rodney wasn't going anywhere.

Tom pulled out his cock. Oh, that felt better. Things had been getting too crowded in his jeans. This cop was really getting him excited. Why hadn't he found a man in uniform before? He leaned over and picked up the hat which had fallen to the floor, and placed it back on the lawman's head. Oh yeah, that looked good. He was glad that he had left the gun belt on the cop and replaced the tie around his neck. He sure was having fun humiliating this cop- and the cop hadn't seen anything yet. Tom pulled on his hard dick as he got closer to the cop. Good, he was getting scared, pushing himself back in the chair, mmmmpppphhhing through the dirty sock tied into his mouth. Tom wondered what thoughts were going through the mind of the cuffed cop.

"You must be enjoying the taste of that sock, Cop," Tom taunted his captive. "How about smelling the other one?"

With that, Tom kicked off his other boot and stripped off his sock. He pulled it taut and tied it over Rodney's nose, not tight enough to cut off his air supply, but covering enough of his nose that it was impossible for him to avoid inhaling the rank odor of Tom's feet.

"How do you like that Cop?" Tom laughed. "Ripe enough for you? Hey, you must like it; I can see that your cock is growing again. I knew that there must be more juice in those balls of yours. We'll take care of that later. Right now, I've got an itch that has to be relieved."

Tom stood back and started stroking himself. Mmm, yes, slow and easy to start off with. Tom was not in a big hurry, but shit…this cop was making him hot, screaming through his gag, struggling away, tied up in his messy uniform. Tom could see the cop making an effort to get loose; the muscles in his thighs were bulging under his grey trousers as he tried to get his spread legs free of the ropes tying them to the back legs of the chair. The blue eyes staring at him with hatred over the sock tied over his nose. Tom started breathing harder.

"Struggle all you want, Cop," Tom chuckled. "You're not going anywhere. You're all tied up and gagged in your uniform. Those cuffs will keep you in place, along with those tightly knotted ropes. No one gets free of my knots. Yeah, yell all you want, Cop. No one can hear you, not with that smelly sock of mine stuffed in your mouth. Too bad you can't see yourself, Cop. Spooge on your face and on your uniform. I bet your buddies would get a kick out of seeing you now, Cop. All tied up and gagged and your cock hard. Not so much a macho cop now, are you? Get ready Officer. You're about to get a load on you."

Rodney snarled into his gag. With every breath he took he inhaled the sweaty stench of his captor's feet. His mouth was filled with the bitter taste of the mate of the sock tied over his nose. He thumped the chair on the floor, rocking back and forth. He could not tear his eyes away from the guy in front of him, pumping on his hard cock, getting ready to shoot. He was vaguely aware of his own dick, poking erect through the fly of his uniform trousers. Every muscle in his body seemed to be crying out in protest against the prolonged bondage. He could feel his thighs and shoulders burning from the unnatural position in which they were tied. Shit, the guy in front of him was getting a glazed look in his eyes; he was huffing and puffing away, bighting down on his lower lip. Guttural groans started coming from the masked man's throat. Rodney stiffened in fearful apprehension. He closed his eyes.

Tom bit down on his lower lip. He was getting closer and closer to cumming. This felt great…he had missed this kind of activity for the past six months. He looked at the cop, whose eyes were closed tight. He slapped him hard across the face.

"Open those blue headlights of yours, Cop," Tom grunted through clenched teeth. "I want you to watch this. If I didn't want you to see this I would have blindfolded you again."

Tom could barely speak he was getting so close. His cock was slick and slimy with pre-cum. He jerked on it harder and harder. So close…oh yeah, here it came. Spurting out like a volcano erupting. Shooting all over the helpless cop. All over his shirt and tie and black leather jacket. Landing on his handsome face and on the shiny brim of his hat. Oh yeah, so hot… Seeing the cop humiliated, listening to him whimper through his sock stuffed mouth. He could see tears start to run down the cop's face, mixing with the spooge. Aww, the poor guy was upset. But…that hard cock was telling a different story. If all of this was so terrible, why was the cop sporting an erection? Tom leaned over, and grabbed the cop by his chin, forcing him to look up into his eyes.

"Was that as good for you as it was for me, Cop?" Tom asked sneeringly. "It must have been. Look at that woody you have."

Tom grabbed Rodney's dick to emphasize his words.

"You have more treats to look forward to, Cop," Tom snarled. "Just give me a little breather. Why, I can feel my cock coming to life again already."

To be continued?

HANGING TALE

By Nicholas Bowman

The police arrested Erik Kagan for violating the federal Asexualization and Assimilation Act just as he was leaving to attend his 21st birthday party.

Erik spent the next year – as well as his 22nd birthday – going from cells to hearings, from prisons to trials, and back again. At the end of the legal process, he was found guilty and sentenced to both death and castration, even though castration was usually omitted when the death penalty was imposed.

His lawyer suggested it might be grounds for appeal or clemency for at least part of the sentence – why kill someone who has already been removed from the gene pool; why castrate someone who soon will be – but he did not hear from his lawyer again. Either the appeals failed, if they were ever filed, or the lawyer was just trying to cheer Erik up.

Which was why, 17 months to the day the police arrested him, Erik was moved from his isolation cell to solitary in Death Row.

Prisoners on Death Row were kept in cells, one wall of which was bars (it also held the door). The other three walls were solid. The cell itself was only deep enough to accommodate the built in cot and wide enough for the sink, toilet and head of the bed.

Prisoners on Death Row were kept naked as well. "You're going to leave this world dressed the same way you entered it," as one guard put it. Erik was oddly glad he spent his days in jail doing burpees and abs work, supplemented by squats and every variation of push-ups he could think of, from narrow grip to hand stand, to have something to do, if not keep in shape.

Even though he wondered why he continued since the time between being moved to Death Row and being executed was two to four weeks, depending upon the number of prisoners condemned to die.

Twenty-five days later, before breakfast, four guards opened the door, one saying, "You're next."

Two of the guards quickly fastened a two-inch wide black leather belt around Erik's waist. His wrists were snapped into the cuffs that dangled from the back of the belt. Just as fast, his ankles were restrained by a pair of manacles connected by a short metal chain.

Pointlessly, the guards forced Erik to march down at a pace that made him trip. Not that is was that long: down the corridor, into the elevator, a short ride two stories down, and into the foyer with three doors. The guards escorted him through the middle door.

Inside was a doctor's office, outfitted for everything from a quick physical to out-patient surgery. Two men were waiting inside. One was an older dignified man wearing a white jacket. The other was dressed in black, including a watch, cap and sunglasses. Both held clipboards with pens attached.

The man in the white jacket spoke. "I am the prison surgeon," he said. "You will be weighed and measured for your execution. Then you will undergo the first part of your sentence before being briefed on what will happen tomorrow."

Erik sighed an unhappy sigh and let himself be lead to the scale. The doctor adjusted the weights and called out, "148."

The man in black jotted the number down on the clipboard.

Instead of lowering the measure to the top of Erik's head, the measure was adjusted to rest just under his chin. "60 inches," the doctor read out, and the man in black recorded that as well.

While the doctor lead Erik back to the examining table, listened to his chest, and took his pulse and blood pressure, the man in black continued to write on his clipboard.

"Well," the doctor said, "you're healthy enough to hang."

The man in black spoke for the first time. It was a slow monotone. "I'll see him in two hours."

"Unless there's a complication," the doctor said.

With that, the man in black left the room.

The guards surrounded Erik and pushed him back onto the examining table. His biceps were strapped to the table, his hands falling into a hollow in the table. Another strap was pulled across his chest.

Meanwhile, two stirrups were pulled out from the table and his ankle manacles removed. His feet were quickly locked into the stirrups and more straps restrained his thighs to the table.

"This won't take long," the doctor said as he washed his hands. "We'll do this under a local. You won't feel a thing."

As he prepared the hypodermic, he continued, "This is buffered Lidocaine. Once the area's numb, we'll open the sac, cut out the testes, sew you back up, and send you over to the hangman. Understood?"

Erik nodded. There wasn't much else to do at that point.

The doctor dabbed the bottom of Erik's sac with an alcohol swab and before Erik could feel the chemical burn, the doctor jabbed the needle into the bottom of the scrotum right into the midline, between Erik's balls.

While the Lidocaine numbed his balls, the doctor quickly shaved Erik's crotch with shaving cream and a straight razor. After the area was shaved smooth, the doctor taped Erik's cock to his lower abdomen.

The doctor then turned his attention back to Erik's sac. The doctor took a large scalpel and cut through both the skin and the subcutaneous tissue, an incision that was an inch and half long and pierced both the inner and outer sacs protecting the ball. Putting aside the blade, he then probed inside the sac and pulled out the left ball. Erik felt the tug behind his abdominal wall. The doctor clamped the spermatic cord.

Next, the doctor picked up a needle and surgical suture. He stitched the cord closed in two places above the clamp. He cut the thread, and picked up another scalpel.

One of the guards sniggered, adding, "This is it."

The doctor silenced the guard with a look.

The doctor turned his attention back to Erik's left ball, kept outside its sac by a clamp, the cords sewn shut in two places. The doctor cut the cord just below the clamp and put Erik's left ball into a metal tray.

He checked the cord for bleeding, released the clamp, and let the cord snap back into the sac.

Just as quickly, he cut off Erik's right ball, completing the prisoner's castration. He finished the operation by closing the incision with an absorbable suture.

As the guards released Erik from the examining table, the doctor said, "Sensation will return in a couple of hours. It will hurt a bit. If you can't deal with that until tomorrow, you may ask for a pain killer."

Erik stared at his balls which were grayish white, looking a little like viscous garlic heads, lying in the metal tray.

"Don't worry about your balls," the doctor said, "there are some body parts we don't use."

The guards then marched Erik back out into the lobby and through the door to the left.

The room was an eighteen foot cube with a platform halfway up and halfway across at the far side. There were doors above and below the platform. Also above the platform was an eyelet centered above a double door a yard square in the middle of the platform. Below the platform was a flight of stairs along the back wall going up to the platform.

The guards marched Erik up the stairs and through a door in the back corner.

The man in black was waiting. He was surrounded by drums of ¾ inch Manila hemp rope and was facing a large boiling cauldron.

"Your rope," he said to Erik," all seventeen feet and seven inches of it."

"So long?" Erik said in astonishment, despite himelf.

"Not that long. To make sure it's not so long that your head's cut off by the speed of the drop or so short that you choke while you're still conscious, we subject your chin height from the distance between the trap and the crossbeam and then add your drop distance, which is determined by your weight, plus seven feet. That's nine minus five plus six-seven plus seven."

"When the rope's the right length, the drop snaps your neck and you go unconscious from medical shock. You won't know or feel anything while you choke to death. You'll be brain dead in about six minutes and your heart will go on for another minute or so. Once the doctor declares you dead, you go into the O.R. and he takes what he needs.

"It's about done now," the man in black said, looking into the pot. "I have to boil the rope to get rid of any bounce, stiffness or coiling it may have. Once it's dry, you'll get to see us test the rope and the trap."

The man in black nodded to the guards who then marched Erik back out the way they came.

The pain, when it came an hour later, was not bad. But his hunger pains were and he had already had his last meal. He wasn't even allowed water. There was none in the chemical toilet and the mains to the cell since had been turned off.

Late in the afternoon, the guards returned for Erik and brought him back to the execution chamber. A noose was now dangling from the eyelet and a couple of large sandbags rested near the trap doors.

The man in black was on a ladder below the platform, oiling the hinges of one of the doors. Finished, he worked his way carefully down the ladder and walked over to where Erik and the guards were waiting.

"Good timing," he said. "We're ready to test the trap. It has to release and stop. We wouldn't want the doors to bounce back and hit you while you drop."

The trap was tested three times, Erik discovered. But each time the test was observed from a different vantage point: on the platform, below the trap, and from the audience's point of view. And as the man in black reset the trapdoors after each test, he said, "Looks like you'll drop free and clear so far."

Next the noose itself was to be tested. The knot had nine coils and was lubricated with paraffin.

"Not that you care, but I appreciate your being a light weight. Seventy-five pound sandbags are heavy enough," the man in black said.

The noose was used to tie the two bags together. The trap was released and the bags dropped through fast and smooth, stopping short, turning, but not bouncing, at the end of the rope.

The noose too was tested from each vantage point. Satisfied with the results the man in black dismissed Erik and the guards.

Back in the cell, Erik found himself alone, too sore, too hungry and too thirsty to exercise to escape thinking about what he didn't want to think about. After a while, he fell into a fitful sleep.

The guards woke him early and marched him over to the prison barber, who not only shaved Erik's jaw, but also the rest of his head. In addition, the barber removed the stubble around Erik's crotch.

Then the guards lead Erik to the shower room, where the attendant sprayed Erik's body – chest, back, arms, legs – with white foam that tingled. After five minutes, the attendant hosed Erik down, leaving him foam free and totally hairless but for his eyebrows and eye lashes.

The guards next brought Erik into the execution chamber, walking him past a gurney with a body bag and toe tag on it, to the stairs to the top of the platform. On the platform, a hooded executioner and his assistant waited. Erik looked out to the audience. It was just the warden and his assistant. No one to say good bye.

The doctor came in. The warden said, "Good. Now we can begin," and mounted the stairs. He kept the legal formalities brief. He reiterated Erik's sentence and then asked the customary question whether there was a particular person or type of person to whom Erik would like to see his organs transplanted. Erik didn't have any such requests, so the warden ordered the execution to proceed.

The guards snapped a two-inch wide black ankle strap with a chrome release around Erik's ankles. The executioner pulled a black hood over Erik's head.

The executioner then lowered the noose over Erik's head and tightened it snugly around Erik's neck, adjusting the knot so that it nestled behind his left ear.

The warden nodded, and the executioner released the trap.

Erik felt the door fall away from his feet, falling and the rope jerking against his neck with a loud snap before he lost all thought and sensation. His arms flared slightly as he fell. His neck angled slightly from the break. His limp body rotated slowly, his cock gradually bloating from the blood no longer reaching his head.

The doctor waited until cum dribbled out of Erik's cock before checking to see if the prisoner was dead. Satisfied, the doctor signaled the guards who rolled over the gurney. The noose was cut and the body laid out on top of the body bag. The hood, noose, and restraints were removed and the toe tag attached. The body bag was zipped up and the guards rolled the gurney out the door, across the foyer and through the third door.

Behind the door was a large room with a couple of operating tables as well as a dozen life support beds. The doctors looked at the chart for organ requests. Noting that the current crop of organ requests, immediate and pending, to keep citizens the state deemed worthy alive would be filled by the stock he had, the doctor called up the medical school and asked them to come over to collect a cadaver for its anatomy class.

THE STORY OF THE RYAN'S

By Christopher Trevor

PROLOGUE

My name is Laura Ryan. About six months ago my husband Mike and I had an awful and life-altering experience that I have come to feel I *must* tell about. I am hoping that my telling of it will prevent it from happening to other people in the future…and hopefully my telling of it will cause my husband to be returned to me. Six months ago my husband Mike and I had gone out to dinner followed by a Broadway show in New York City. It was a warm Saturday evening in mid June. After the show we walked slowly hand in hand through the crowded streets of Manhattan toward the train station, heading for home. I was dressed in a black knee-length skirt, a white blouse, black stockings, and black high-heeled pumps. My handsome husband was wearing an olive-colored suit, a white shirt, a silk patterned necktie, well shined black lace-up wingtips and black calf-length nylon dress socks. Always the handsome businessman that husband of mine. When we reached forty-Ninth Street we walked slowly down the steps of the subway station. We were in the back section of the station, when we actually needed to be in the front. I told this to Mike but he said not to worry, that we would simply walk to the front of the station when we were downstairs. I told him that that scared me because the back end of that particular train station was almost always deserted. Again Mike told me not to worry as we walked the rest of the way down the stairs. Sure enough, the area around the token booth was deserted, silent, and almost as silent as a tomb. There wasn't even a clerk in the token booth. Mike noticed this as well and said that it was fortunate he always carried extra tokens (this was in the days before the invention of the Metro-Card) with him. He reached into his suit pants pocket and took out two tokens, handing one to me. We went through the turnstiles and onto the deserted platform to wait for the Brooklyn bound "N" train.

"It's so quiet down here," I said to Mike. "It's almost scary…funny how its so desolate down here and yet right above us are thousands of people walking the streets."

"Don't worry," my husband said reassuringly. "I ride the trains' everyday."

"So do I, but that's during rush-hour when it's crowded," I said.

"Let's walk to the front end of the platform," Mike said. "I'm sure it won't be as deserted there."

As we began walking we were passing a door with a sign on it that read "Porter's Room." Suddenly, the door was thrown open and three men, all dressed in jeans, flannel shirts and construction worker style boots stepped out in front of us, blocking our way, and blocking the view of us from any other passengers who might have been in the front area of the train station.

"Well, well, well, and just what the fuck do we have here?" the first man said, looking at Mike and I hungrily. "Nice, *real fucking nice…*"

Mike slipped an arm around me, said excuse me in an authoritative tone of voice, and tried to walk us past the three mean and very street looking men. What Mike didn't realize was that his authoritative voice works in the office with his underlings, but when it came to these three street thugs that voice of authority meant nothing. As we tried to move past the three men they again blocked our path. They all looked pretty muscular, they all had sloppy and unkempt facial hair and they were all sadistic and sinister looking at the same time.

"Look, we don't want any trouble, okay?" Mike said to the first man who seemed to be the ringleader. "Just let us get by and we'll be on our way."

The three men didn't move. They simply stood there smiling fiendishly at us.

"Look, what is it you want?" Mike asked nervously, though trying at the same time to sound brave. "Money?"

"Yeah sure, money would be nice, but I can think of something even better," the first man said to us.

Mike pulled me closer to himself, trying to shield me from them.

"Now look, you can have our money, but leave my wife alone," Mike said to the first man.

"HA, it ain't your wife we want Handsome…" the first man said in an icy tone of voice, looking lustfully at my handsome husband.

Mike's face turned pale white. Suddenly, we were grabbed and pulled violently away from each other. The first man and the one standing next to him grabbed Mike by his upper arms and wrenched them behind him. Mike grunted loudly in pain and swore at the two men like a sailor. The third man grabbed me in a bear-like grip and yanked my arms behind me as well. As I screamed Mike struggled helplessly in the two men's grasps. My screams echoed through the train station but no one came to help. This is New York we're talking about here after all. The first man told his friends to follow him as he moved toward the door marked "Porter's Room." I watched helplessly as Mike was practically lifted off his feet and half carried half dragged into the room. The man holding onto me followed the other men, dragging me with him into the room as well. As the door slammed shut behind us I heard the train that we should have been getting on roar into the station.

IN THE ROOM

The porter's room was fairly large, lit by three big bare bulbs hanging from the ceiling. The room was filled mostly with mops, brooms and water buckets. On shelves I saw cans of disinfectant, sprays, and other cleaning utensils such as scrub-brushes and work-gloves. Mike struggled like a madman to pull free from the two men holding him tight and fast but it was totally useless. As strong and as built as my husband was he was no match for the two men. He was forced to watch as the man holding onto me clamped a burly arm around my mid-section (pinning my arms down) and a hand around my neck.

"ACCCCCHHHH…" I rasped as he slightly choked me.

"Okay Handsome, stop the fucking struggling or my buddy over there will strangle the life out of her," the first man said viciously into Mike's ear.

Mike was stunned as the man gave his ear a wet slurpy lick. Mike stopped struggling and looked across at me helplessly.

"All right, just don't hurt her…" Mike pleaded. "Do anything, but don't hurt her…"

"That was the plan from the get-go…" the first man said to Mike, holding his arm tighter and tighter in his firm grasp.

He then looked over at the man holding me.

"Tie the bitch to the post so she can watch," the thug ordered, then looked menacingly at Mike. "I want her to watch every second of this…she is not going to believe her damned eyes…"

Mike watched as the man walked me over to a wooden post in the center of the room. He yanked my hands behind me and around the post and proceeded to rope them behind me, binding me to the post.

"What is this all about???" Mike angrily asked the ringleader.

"This is about you..." the ringleader said, and again licked Mike's ear, giving his earlobe a quick suck.

"FUCKING FAGGOTS!!!" Mike screamed as the realization of their plans flooded his mind and he stomped hard on the ringleader's foot.

"UFFFFF!!!" the ringleader grunted and let go of Mike's arm.

With his free hand Mike made a fist and punched the second man hard across the face.

"UNNNNGHHH..." the second man blurted in shock, let go of Mike's other arm, and fell against a wall.

When Mike turned to me he saw to his dismay that the third man had his huge hand around my throat again.

"Don't come any closer man!" the third man said threateningly to Mike. "I swear, I will kill her!"

Mike stood there shaking with anger, his fists clenched, undecided it seemed about what to do. From behind him the first and second men grabbed him by his upper arms again. They held him tight and I saw the look of defeat that came over his handsome face.

"Bastards!!" Mike yelled.

"You best do as we tell you Handsome," the first man said, leering at Mike from the side, his tongue practically hanging out as he spoke. "If not I will let my good buddy over there kill your damned wife...I'll make you watch as he slowly strangles her."

"D-do what you want and just get it the fuck over with!!" Mike ranted angrily.

Smiling across at each other the two men holding Mike's arms let go of them and helped him off with his suit jacket, tossing it to the floor. They proceeded to run their big hands over Mike's crisp white shirt, tugging on his tie. They slapped at his chest really hard and squeezed his muscular arms.

"*Bastards…*" Mike whispered through clenched teeth as the two men pawed and handled him. "*Fucking turds…*"

The second man stepped in front of my husband and slowly undid the knot in Mike's tie. He slid the tie off Mike and began unbuttoning Mike's shirt, slowly revealing my handsome husband's somewhat hairy chest and two beefy nipples.

"Looks like your dear hubby is having fun," the man holding me and clutching my throat said tauntingly.

Anger filled me.

"Mike, don't let them do this!!" I suddenly shrieked. "Don't worry about me, just stop them!! This is all so sick!!" As Mike's shirt was pulled off him he looked over at me. The man holding me quickly tightened his hand on my throat again.

"Don't even think about it man," the third man said to my husband. "You just keep doing that strip for us and everything will be fine…"

"Put your hands up behind your head so the lady can watch what happens next," the first man said to Mike.

Mike did as he was told and lifted his arms, crossing his hands behind his head, revealing the thick tufts of hair in his deep armpits. He stood there bare-chested, wearing just the bottom portion of his suit. The two men ran their hands over Mike's muscular and well-toned chest, his flat stomach; they squeezed his beefy brown nipples a few times and toyed with the thick tufts of his armpit hair.

"Nice Handsome, real fucking nice…" the first man said lustfully and sniffed Mike's armpits while squeezing one of his nipples.

Mike grimaced as he was handled.

The second man gave Mike's flat stomach and muscular pecs a few hard slaps and said that my husband sure could take it.

"Perverts…" Mike seethed. "Fucking degenerates you guys are…"

The first man picked up Mike's tie and pulled my husband's arms and hands behind him. He began tying Mike's hands behind himself.

"You-you don't have to tie me up," Mike pleaded. "I-I swear, I won't try anything…"

"What's the matter Handsome, afraid we're going to ruin your expensive silk tie?" the second man asked Mike tauntingly as he squeezed my husband's nipples real hard.

"AARRRRHHHH…shit…" Mike seethed angrily as the man twisted his nipples and meanly pinched them.

When Mike's hands were securely tied behind him the first and second men each leaned down a bit and took one of my husband's nipples into their mouth. They began loudly sucking, chewing and bighting on Mike's nubs.

"OHHHHHHHHH FUCK!!! You bastards!!!" Mike ranted.

"These tits of yours ain't all we're going to suck Handsome," the second man said in between slurps on my poor husband's nipples.

As Mike's nipples were really being tortured after a while I heard a train enter the station on the opposite platform. All those people out there and no one to help Mike or rescue him from what I knew to be an impending fate.

"Hey, get the fuck over here and join us," the first man said to the man standing next to me. "With his hands safely tied behind him he ain't going to do anything…"

The third man grinned, looked at me fiendishly, and walked over to join his two friends. The first man took his mouth off Mike's nipple and invited the third man to work on it. The second man hadn't once stopped working Mike's other nipple since he had sucked it into his greedy mouth. The first man stepped behind my husband, placed the palms of his hands on Mike's big biceps, leaned forward, and kissed Mike on the back of his neck. Mike looked over at me helplessly. Tears flowed from my eyes as my husband grunted in pain as the second and third men continued to torture his nipples with their mouths.

"Fucking beautiful hunk you are..." the first man said directly into my husband's ear and kissed him again on the back of his neck.

"Fuckers..." Mike said angrily through clenched teeth.

Laughing almost fiendishly like some sort of old fashioned movie villain the first man ran his big tongue back and forth over the back of Mike's neck, rubbing his broad shoulders at the same time.

When the second and third men finally stopped sucking on Mike's nipples they looked all sore, red, and painfully erect. The first man stopped licking Mike's neck and told his two buddies that he wanted to finish undressing my husband. Mike turned to him angrily as the second man unbuckled his belt.

"You fucking bastards!!" Mike yelled in the man's face. "What's the point of all this??"

As the first man smiled and stroked my husband's hair Mike's suit pants fell down embarrassingly around his ankles, revealing his white BVD briefs and the big beefy bulge he was sporting in them.

"Fuck man, look at that!!" the second man exclaimed loudly. "He's got a fucking hard-on!! Handsome hunk bastard is really enjoying all this shit after all!!"

The first man held Mike balanced by his upper arms as the second and third men quickly squatted down and pulled Mike's suit pants off him over his shoes and socks.

"You fucking perverts!!" Mike said angrily.

But there was no denying it. Mike did have an erection in his briefs. Even from where I was standing across the room I could see it. Mike had a real big Irish-sized dick, if ever there was one…all thick, long and what the porn people would call, beefy. His Irish sausage was what he and I jokingly called it… Seeing him standing there with that man-sized bulge in his briefs at that moment made me suddenly and unbelievably…horny.

My husband stood there helplessly in his white briefs, black shoes and black socks as the second and third men squatted at his sides, running their hands up and down his muscular legs, caressing and squeezing them.

"Nice sexy legs Handsome, real fucking nice…" the second man said and nuzzled his nose and mouth against Mike's briefs.

"I do not believe this shit!!" Mike said to me from across the room.

"And you thought it was your wife we were after Handsome," the first man said, grabbed Mike's chin, and forcefully turned my husband's face to him.

The guy kissed Mike hard on the mouth, ferociously forcing his tongue deep into Mike's mouth.

"RRRRRmmmmmmfffff!!!" Mike screamed in protest.

When the first man released Mike's mouth he looked down at his two friends.

"Yeah, lick those under shorts of his you two…fuckin' suck on his damned briefs!!" he commanded.

The two men did as they were told. The first man hooked his hand tightly around Mike's arm, placed his other hand behind Mike's neck, and pulled his face close to him. This time it seemed Mike accepted the kiss with no protest. I heard another train enter the station and when I looked again at my husband the second man had taken Mike's dick out of the fly opening in his briefs. I watched in horror as the second man slurped my husband's big, throbbing dick into his mouth and began sucking on it. Mike quickly pulled his mouth away from the first man's mouth and looked down, also in horror.

"OHHHHHH no, no, not this man!!" Mike groaned miserably. "Fucking pervert is sucking my damned dick!!"

The first man grinned maniacally at my husband, ran his hands gently over Mike's chest, and took a few steps back to watch as my bound husband stood there wearing just his underpants, his shoes and socks, and had his dick sucked like crazy…by a man. Mike looked up at me in utter despair.

"Enjoy it man," the third man said to Mike.

He was still squatting next to Mike, stealing licks off Mike's briefs. Watching all this I found myself angered shocked and amazingly, somehow turned on all at once. The first man again stepped behind Mike and kissed and licked the back of my husband's neck. He placed his hands under Mike's briefs and gave my husband's buns a few squeezes.

"*Ooooohhhhhhh GOD, you fuckers…*" Mike screamed as he stood there sweating, having his big Irish sausage sucked, his briefs licked, and his buns squeezed.

It was obvious, even to me, that Mike *was* turned on by all this, yet furious and feeling utterly violated at the same time. The second man stopped sucking Mike's dick and the third man quickly took over, gobbling my husband's dick into his mouth.

"UHHHHHNNNN…" Mike grunted. "You too huh?"

The first man let go of Mike's buns and reached around my husband's chest. He took Mike's nipples in his thumbs and first fingers and squeezed them, twisting them hard.

"Goin' to shoot a load soon huh Handsome?" the first man taunted Mike as he toyed with his nipples.

"BAS-Bastard!!" Mike seethed. "I'm-I'm fucking getting there now!! But I don't believe this shit!!"

The third man quickly took Mike's dick out of his mouth, grabbed it in his hand, held it tight and pointed it straight down as Mike shot a big hefty load of cum onto his well-shined wingtips.

"OHHHHHHHH...OHHHHHHHHHH!!!" Mike screamed in a man's passion. "Fuck, I am cumming!! I-I'm sorry Laura!!"

Mike's cum splattered all over his shoes and some dripped onto the sides of his socks.

"Looks like you two have a tasty treat," the first man said to his two friends.

The first man let go of Mike's nipples and he grabbed Mike's upper arms as the other two men grabbed one of his legs each. Together, all three men lifted my muscular husband up off the floor.

"Bastards!!" Mike yelled. *"Put me the fuck down!!!"*

They sat Mike on top of a table and dangled his long legs off the end of it. The second and third men each squatted at one of Mike's feet, and, holding him by his calves they proceeded to lick Mike's cum off his shoes and socks...really sucking and slurping at them.

"GODDAMNED PERVERTS!!" Mike yelled at the two men. "FUCKING DEGENERATES..."

As the second and third men licked my husband's shoes and socks the first man stood next to him, stroking his soft wavy brown hair. He turned Mike's face to him and again kissed him on the mouth.

"I sure as all fuck do love kissin' you Handsome," the first man said passionately. "Your lips taste so fucking good..."

With that he kissed Mike again and then looked over at me.

"You enjoying all this Honey Bunch?" the first man asked me mockingly. "Bet by now you're wishing it was you getting this treatment..."

"Leave him alone already!!" I hollered across the room.

But instead the man smiled fiendishly, turned to Mike, pushed my husband down on the table, and pushed his big tongue again into Mike's mouth. I wasn't sure but it looked like Mike opened his mouth to receive the kiss with no resistance. The first man kissed Mike over and over, stroking his hair and rubbing his chest at the same time. By now the second and third men had finished licking all of Mike's cum off his shoes and socks. My husband's dick was still sticking out of his briefs, dangling long and semi-erect against the white cotton material. Seeing his dick like that sent a strange feeling chill through me. In our sex lives Mike and I never really ventured into the kinky aspect of things. We always stripped down naked, never left undergarments on, never licked our fluids off thin materials, and we never ventured into the bondage arena. Watching Mike being sexed over by three men was killing me…yet somehow arousing me at the same time. I felt like I was cheating in a way…hating myself yet not able to control the lust that seemed to be building in me. The men sat Mike up on the table and together all three of them rubbed his chest, squeezed his muscular arms, pinched his nipples, and ran their hands over his broad shoulders. They tauntingly called him names such as Handsome, Hot guy, and Sexy boy. Mike cursed and swore at them like a captured marine as they nipped and kissed his nipples…but a while later my husband's dick was fully hard yet again, still sticking temptingly out of his briefs. My God, what was it about seeing my husband's dick like that that was driving me wild inside? I mean, even though he was suffering miserably and humiliatingly at the moment I was aroused beyond comprehension.

"Looks like we'll get another good load out of him," the second man exclaimed happily.

Mike looked at him in a mixture of despair and anger.

"Later for that," the first man said with total authority. "Right now it's our turn to cum…get those briefs off him…*now!!*"

"NO, oh God, no!!" Mike ranted and trembled in total fear as the three men ripped his briefs off him.

When his briefs were off him the men yanked my husband off the table, slumped him over it, and forcefully pushed his long muscular legs as far apart as possible.

"OH GOOD GOD NO!!!" Mike cried. *"No!!!"*

Tears of rage streamed down my face now as the first man crammed Mike's ripped up briefs into his mouth, gagging him. Mike struggled like mad to get his hands untied as the first man stepped behind him but it was useless. His hands were tied too tight…and so were mine. The first man took his big monster-sized dick out of the fly opening in his jeans. His dick was big, fat, and even from where I was standing, I could see that it was throbbing. The man placed his hands on Mike's butt cheeks and spread them. Mike whimpered helplessly behind his gag.

"Leave him alone you bastard!!!" I suddenly screamed in rage. *"Stop this already, MY GOD, stop this!!!"*

The first man looked over at me, smiled, and gave Mike's butt a fast slap. He then plunged his dick into my husband's anal opening all at once.

"RRRMMMMMFFFF!!!!" Mike wailed in agony.

"Oh yeah, nice and tight you are!!" the first man said as he began to thrust in and out of Mike's hole.

The second and third men laughed hysterically as the first man viciously fucked my poor husband.

"YOU bastard!!!" I screamed. *"Help us!!! Someone help us!!!"*

I was screaming in the direction of the door for the porter's room, but of course there was no one to hear me and the three men knew that. They gagged me anyway. As the first man mercilessly fucked and raped Mike he spanked my husband's butt cheeks hard…the sound sharp and filling the room. Mike grunted in pain behind his gag. When the first man was about to cum he pulled his dick out of Mike's hole and shot his load all over Mike's ass cheeks.

"OH yeah!! YEAH!!!" he grunted. "Fuckin' hot hole you got there Handsome!!"

When he was done he stepped out of the way and the second man took his place. Mike watched in horror, his head craned around, as the second man pulled his dick from his jeans. It was also big and fat like the first man's. Mike squeezed his tear-filled eyes shut as the second man plunged his dick into his hole. As the second man fucked my husband he ran the palms of his hands over Mike's cum smeared ass cheeks, massaging them, digging his fingers roughly into them.

"OH YEAH, hot ass is right!!" the second man panted breathlessly.

He stood straight up behind Mike, thrusting his big spear-like dick in and out of my husband's hole. Mike writhed miserably on the table. The first man sauntered over to me with a fiendish looking smile on his face. His dick was still hanging grossly out of his pants…droplets of pre cum oozing on the tip of it.

"Your handsome hubby sure can take it…" he said to me, sounding totally lecherous. "You should consider yourself lucky to have such a guy around the house."

I looked at the first man with utter hatred showing in my eyes. I wondered if my husband would ever be the same after this.

"He's so fucking hot that I may just fuck him again before we let you two go…" he said, running his hand over his hardening dick. "Or maybe, just maybe, when we leave here we'll take your handsome stud of a husband with us…and keep him as a sex slave…"

I looked at him in total and utter disbelief as he spoke. He *could not be serious.*

"You would never see your handsome hubby again…" he whispered insanely, looking at me intently, no longer smiling now.

Suddenly, the first man's words were cut off as the second man announced breathlessly that he was cumming. Unlike the first man he shot his load directly into Mike's hole.

"OH YEAAAHHHHH!!!" the second man moaned as he came and came inside my poor husband.

He thrust his dick hard into Mike's hole as he shot and shot his load...

He spanked my husband's butt cheeks hard as he seemed to just cum and cum and cum like crazy into Mike's hole.

"YEAHHH!!! FUCK YEAH!!!" the second man grunted.

Mike raised his head off the table, turned, and looked at the second man with hate-filled eyes.

"Oh yeah, greased up your hole real good Handsome!!" the second man said as his dick slid out of Mike's hole.

From where I was standing I was able to see that Mike's hole had been brutally stretched and was indeed moist all over with the second man's cum. The second man had remnants of his cum dripping from his flaccid dick. But then my view of my husband's hole was gone when the third man stepped behind him and took his hard dick out of his pants. Poor Mike laid his head back down on the table, tears streaming from his eyes.

"Mmm..." I moaned, looking beseechingly at the first man who was still standing next to me.

"Want us to stop huh?" the first man asked me. "Probably thinking he can't take anymore huh?"

I nodded my head "yes" as tears flowed from my eyes as well.

"When we grabbed you two you probably thought we wanted you right pretty lady?" the first man asked me. "That it was you we wanted to gang rape and torment the fuck out of, right? Do all that we're doing to your stud husband while he watched, RIGHT?"

I nodded "yes" again and at that moment Mike screamed in pain behind his gag as the third man plunged his dick into his hole.

"We like women…we like women a lot…" the first man explained to me. "But, quite honestly baby, there is no fucking thing like a guy screaming and grunting in pain while he's being worked over like your handsome hubby is being worked over right now."

We both looked over and saw the look of utter pain, agony and total humiliation on Mike's face as his ass was fucked a third time.

"Oh yeah, I have to fuck him again!" the first man said. "YO!!! Hurry the fuck up and cum man!! I want another fucking go at him!!"

The first and second men laughed hysterically as I heard another train enter the station. A while later the third man shot his load into Mike's hole also. When he was done the men helped Mike off the table and to a standing position.

Mike was crying in a man's pain, shuddering and whimpering behind his gag.

"Oh yeah Hot guy!!" the first man said, running a hand over Mike's chest and slapping it hard. "I bet you're feeling real good now eh? Some tough topnotch business guy you are, allowing the three of us to capture you, strip you and fuck your ass like you were some cheap whore! HA!!!"

He slapped Mike's chest again.

"MMMMMFFF!!!!" Mike grunted loudly at the man, spittle flying from the sides of his gagged mouth.

All the men proceeded to run their hands over Mike's body, exploring him everywhere. They squeezed his poor sore nipples over and over till they looked like they were beyond sore…then they gave them a few hard sucks and slurps each.

"Okay Handsome, now I want another go at that sweet hole of yours, and then we'll decide what the fuck we're going to do with you," the first man said.

Mike did not struggle as they slumped him back over the table, spreading his legs apart again. Mike's hole was open, exposed, stretched, and ready as the first man stepped behind him. Mike uttered a loud grunt of pain as the first man plunged his hard dick into his hole. My husband was viciously fucked a fourth time.

"OH yeah, yeah!!" the first man moaned, slapping Mike's butt cheeks hard.

The two other men cheered him on as they packed their dicks back into their pants. When the first man shot his load he did so into my husband's hole, digging his big fingers into Mike's butt cheeks at the same time, and screaming loud in sick and twisted ecstasy. When he was done his dick slipped out of Mike's hole and he packed it back into his pants. The second man yanked Mike's ripped briefs out of his mouth.

"FU-FUCKING bastards..." Mike whimpered miserably.

The second man pushed Mike's legs together and pulled my husband's dick and balls out from behind his thighs. Mike's dick was hard and his balls were bulging, twitching and hanging low. All three of the men squatted behind my husband and took turns sucking Mike's dick, they licked his balls, and ran their tongues over his butt cheeks. They ran their hands over Mike's shoes and socks, toying with them as they slowly forced Mike toward a second orgasm of his own. I was wet as a sponge...

"OHHHHHHHH..." Mike moaned. "You guys, fucking passing my dick around like it was a damned joint!"

As the second man sucked Mike's dick the first and third men each bit on Mike's butt cheeks."AAARRRGHHHHH...easy guys...easy..." Mike grunted as he pulled himself to his toes and shot his load into the second man's mouth. "OHHHHHHHHHHH..."

The second man swallowed every drop of Mike's second load. When he was done he let Mike's dick slip out of his mouth, smacking his lips together happily. All three men stood up and together they hauled Mike up off the table to a standing position. Mike's dick flopped back in front of himself along with his tortured balls. He stood still and exhausted, in pain, as the three men kissed his nipples, his chest, and shoulders. The called him Hot guy and Handsome over and over. Mike looked across the room at me in disbelief.

"Get over there with his bitch wife," the first man said to the third man.

The third man did as he was told; he came over to me and looked menacingly at Mike.

"Y-you said you wouldn't hurt her…" Mike said pleadingly to the first man.

"I just want to make sure you keep doing as you're told Handsome," the first man said to Mike as he ran his fingers through my husband's hair.

He untied Mike's hands and Mike massaged his wrists. I watched as the first man handed Mike his ripped briefs.

"Get dressed," he said to Mike.

"Look, you got what you wanted," Mike said, holding his ripped briefs in his hand and looking at the men helplessly. "Just let us go now, okay?"

The man grabbed Mike's nipples in his fingers and squeezed them hard.

"OHHHHHHHH AAARRGHHHH!!!" Mike grunted loudly through clenched teeth as the man squeezed and twisted his sore nipples. "AAAYYYRRRR SHHIIITTT!!!"

"I said to get dressed!!" the man barked loudly.

He let go of Mike's nipples and with his hands trembling Mike pulled on his ripped briefs. I watched as Mike put on his shirt and with his fingers trembling even more-so he buttoned it up. He looked at me nervously.

Obviously he had heard the first man mention taking him with them to be their sex slave. *Could he have meant it???* I trembled as Mike pulled his pants on, tucking his shirt into them. Moments later Mike was fully dressed in his suit.

"Lookin' good Handsome," the first man said and mockingly straightened Mike's tie.

"Y-you are going to let us go now, right?" Mike asked the first man.

The first and second men each grabbed one of Mike's arms.

"Handsome guy, I cannot imagine being without you," the first man said menacingly.

"Me either," the second man said.

Holding Mike tightly by his arms they walked him over to me. The third man pulled my gag off me and Mike and I looked at each other helplessly.

"Say good-bye you two," the first man said commandingly.

"Th-this can't be happening…" Mike said to me, utter fear showing in his eyes. *"I-I'm being kidnapped Laura…*Bastards raped me…n-now they're kidnapping me…"

Trembling like a leaf in a windstorm, Mike leaned forward to kiss me, but the first man yanked him back by a handful of his hair.

"OWWWWW!!!" Mike roared.

"I said to say good-bye," the first man seethed. "I do not recall giving you permission to kiss her!! The only ones you'll be kissing from now on are us!!"

"B-but she's my wife!!" Mike yelled at the man.

"You're my wife now Handsome!!" the first man replied.

I screamed Mike's name over and over as the first and second men led him out the door of the room we were in. The third man loosened the ropes around my wrists, and laughing sadistically, ran out of the room after his friends.

"MIKE!!!!" I screamed louder as I quickly pulled my hands free of the loosened ropes.

Shaking, I ran out of the room and onto the subway platform. As it was earlier it was deserted. Only now I was alone.

"*Mike!!!*" I screamed, my voice echoing through the station. "*Oh my God, Mike!!!*"

On the floor I saw Mike's gold wedding band. I picked it up and stood there sobbing, the ring clutched in my trembling fist.

EPILOGUE - SIX MONTHS LATER

It has now been six months since my husband Mike was taken from me... literally hauled off by those three rapists. The police don't have any leads and a private detective I hired has come up with nothing pertaining to Mike's whereabouts. It's as if the three men who took him never existed. Even sketches that were done by police artists based on descriptions I gave them turned up nothing. At night I lay awake thinking, imagining what those sadistic bastards must be doing to my poor husband. Other nights I lay awake wondering if Mike is even still alive. Mike's manager at the bank phoned me after a month to tell me that the company had been forced at that point to replace him. By company policy he told me that they could not hold a person's job if the person did not report absence within an adequate amount of time. Somewhere out there my husband is being tortured and repeatedly raped by those men... I wonder if I will ever see Mike again...

Recently, on a Saturday afternoon I was out shopping in Manhattan. I needed to finally get out and start doing normal everyday things. As I was waiting for the light to change so I could cross the street I saw a motorcycle moving slowly behind some cars. Two men were on the motorcycle, both of them dressed all in black...the one sitting on the back of the motorcycle had his arms wrapped tightly around the man driving the motorcycle. As I stood there the man on the back of the motorcycle saw me. He seemed to be looking at me through the visor of his motorcycle helmet. Being that his visor was tinted black I could not see the man's face. The driver however did not have a tinted visor on his helmet and he looked eerily familiar. My heart raced when I noticed that the man on the back of the motorcycle had a shackle locked around his ankle which was connected to the motorcycle by a short chain. I had heard about the relationships between some S&M fetishists, so it seemed reasonable that no one would think it strange that the man on the back of the motorcycle was shackled to it. But still... The driver of the motorcycle saw me looking, stepped hastily on the starter, and as soon as the light changed to green, sped off... I stood there trembling... and wondering...

EDDIE

By Christopher Trevor

I've worked with Eddie for a few years now and I have to admit that I always found him to be attractive. Eddie is a handsome black man; he's about five feet seven inches tall. He has brown eyes and a decent body. When I noticed that he was starting to look broader around the shoulders and chest areas I asked him if he had been working out. He said that he had indeed been working out; going on to explain that he had bought a set of weights complete with a bench and chin-up bar. Every night he worked out at home for at least an hour or more. As Eddie's body became more and more muscular I became more and more attracted to him. His white dress shirts for work started showing the outline of the muscles on his arms, shoulders and chest. Sometimes I could see his nipples pressing against his shirt. It drove me wild. I love tits, I love big muscles, and the combination of the two is mesmerizing to me. One day during the workweek about a year or so ago I complimented Eddie on his body and added that I wished I could learn to workout with weights. As luck would have it Eddie invited me over to his apartment after work that night. I thanked him but told him that I had no workout clothes with me. Eddie said that was no big deal at all, suggesting that we could just work out in our underwear. We were two guys who'd been in locker rooms before after all. Workout in our underwear I thought. It was more than obvious that this guy was cock teasing me. Eddie knew that I was gay and probably wanted to show off his magnificent body in front of me just to frustrate me. I had a sudden idea on how to turn the tables on conniving Eddie. With that in mind I agreed to his offer. The workday would not end soon enough for me that day. Finally, at five o'clock, dressed in our suits, Eddie and I took a number two train to his apartment where he lived in Brooklyn. When we got to his apartment we shucked off our suit jackets, ties and white dress shirts. Before we could strip all the way down to our underwear Eddie wanted to show me the weights, the bench, and chin-up bar. Dressed in white tee shirts and the lower portion of our suits we walked to Eddie's spare bedroom. The set of weights <u>was </u>great, complete with a long cushioned bench and a bar across the top of it.

"Wow, this is awesome!!" I said as I took in the sight of the workout equipment.

"Glad you like it," Eddie replied. "Maybe if you enjoy the workout I'm going to give you you'll decide to buy your own set of weights."

I watched as Eddie pulled off his tee shirt. His chest was huge with two big brown nipples pointing off it.

"I'm going to enjoy the workout I'm going to give you even more my friend…" I said to myself.

His shoulders and arms were totally muscular and magnificent. My breath caught in my throat. Already he was enjoying cock teasing me.

"Well, we may as well get started," Eddie said to me.

In moments we were both stripped to our white briefs and dress socks. Eddie wore blue nylon calf length socks and mine were black nylon calf length. I watched as Eddie reached down and folded down the tops of his socks. For some reason with his socks folded down near his ankles it made Eddie look even sexier, vulnerable somehow.

"I usually start by doing three sets of chin-ups," Eddie explained, directing my attention to the chin-up bar which was attached to the wall entrance to the spare bedroom.

It was just below the ceiling.

"Perfect…" I thought happily.

"How many is a set?" I asked Eddie.

"Twelve," Eddie said as we walked to the chin-up bar.

"So that means I'll do thirty reps all together," Eddie went on as he explained. "You can start with one set if you want."

"Okay," I said with a smile.

Eddie jumped up and grabbed the bar with two hands. He closed his hands around the bar, crossed his legs under himself, and hoisted himself up.

"You can spot me by holding my legs crossed for me," he said as he lifted his chin over the bar.

"Okay," I said, trying not to sound too anxious.

I stepped behind Eddie and grabbed his calves, my hands on his socks. He lifted himself up and down slowly, counting each rep. His ass looked totally hot in his sweaty white briefs. I could have pressed my face right against his briefs in the back at that moment and inhaled his sexy ass odor. But I wanted to wait. My opportunity would come. I held my hands against Eddie's blue socks, my thumbs pressing hard against the nylon material. When Eddie was in the middle of his second set of chin-ups he started really sweating. I could see it glistening on his beautiful black skin. I wanted at that moment more than anything to lick that sweat off him. When he finished his second set he let himself hang freely, his legs uncrossed.

"One more set…" Eddie said, breathing heavily.

I grabbed Eddie's calves and crossed his legs for him.

"Let's see if you can do two more sets Eddie," I said, hoisting him up.

His chin went over the bar and he slowly lowered himself back down.

"You're on," Eddie said through clenched teeth. "It won't be easy, but I'll do it..."

I held onto Eddie's calves to keep him from uncrossing them as he hoisted himself up again over the chin-up bar. He let out a loud macho sounding groan and called me a would be sadistic personal trainer as he lowered himself. I was there to hoist him up and over though once more...and again...and again...and again...

When Eddie was done he had done a total of forty-eight chin-ups. He stood in front of me massaging his muscular arms, his entire body drenched in sweat.

"Okay Chris, your turn..." Eddie said.

I jumped up and grabbed the bar. Eddie stepped behind me, grabbed my calves as I crossed my legs, and spotted me as I had done for him. I did one set of chin-ups, twelve reps only. When I was done I told Eddie that I would never be able to match his four sets.

"In time you will..." Eddie said. "If you workout regularly like I do that is..."

To show off Eddie jumped up and grabbed the chin-up bar again. He did another set. I watched in awe, knowing that his arms would soon be exhausted. It was then that I took notice of Eddie's armpits. They were deep and extremely hairy. The black thick hair in his pits was matted with sweat. A thought went racing through my mind. Eddie finished with the chin-up bar and I walked with him over to the weight bench.

"Okay, we'll start with biceps and then move on to chest, okay?" Eddie asked me.

"Whatever you say," I replied.

Eddie sat down on the bench, his muscular tree-trunk like legs on the sides of it. He picked up two twenty-five pound dumbbells, leaned forward, and began doing biceps curls.

"Okay, like with the chin-up bar I'll do three sets of this also..." Eddie grunted.

"Okay," I said.

Boy oh boy was Eddie's arms going to be tired. Perfect for what I had in mind. As Eddie did his biceps curls I marveled over the muscles in his huge arms. I glanced over at my suit pants which were on the floor right near the weight bench. Perfect. Eddie finished his three sets and then I took his place on the bench. I did one set of biceps curls and then Eddie set up the bar across the top of the bench. I helped him pile some round weights onto the bar and lock them in place. In total there was eighty pounds on the bar. Eddie lay down on the bench and gripped the weight bar with both hands.

"Okay, stand behind me and spot me by keeping your hands under mine," Eddie instructed me.

"Okay," I said.

God, he looked magnificent lying there like that, all stretched out like a side of beef. Eddie's body was a work of art. He lifted the bar off the bench and brought it over his nipples area. He hefted it up and then slowly brought it back down. He grunted like crazy and was sweating like crazy by then. I could see the outlines of Eddie's cock in his white briefs. He was semi hard. My breath came in short gasps.

"Three sets?" I asked him.

"Yeah, and then it'll be time for a break..." Eddie said through clenched teeth. "My arms are killing me now...by the time I'm done with my third set they'll be in definite need of a rest..."

Just what I was counting on. Eddie grunted and swore his way through his third set. I quickly moved my suit pants closer to myself. It was almost time to teach Eddie a lesson for cock teasing me. His chest looked magnificent as he lifted the bar up and down. When he was done he placed the bar on the top of the bench. He was breathing heavily.

"Damn good," I said, congratulating him.

"Thanks," he replied. "Now it's your turn…"

"Do one more set," I said. "Just to test those arms…"

I quickly reached into my suit pants pocket and took out two pairs of open handcuffs, unseen by Eddie. He gripped the bar and as he was about to lift it I quickly placed the open cuff around one of his wrists, closing it quickly, locking it.

"H-hey!!!" Eddie said in total surprise.

Before he could pull his other hand away I locked the other cuff around his other wrist.

"What the hell are you doing?" Eddie asked me in anger.

I grabbed the other pair of handcuffs and looped one cuff around the chain in the center of the handcuffs on Eddie's wrists and locked the other cuff around the weight bar. Eddie was now tethered to the weight bar.

"Shit…" Eddie rasped. "What are you doing man???"

"It's time to workout my way now Eddie," I said, looking at him lustfully.

"Holy shit man, what are you going to do to me???" Eddie asked, sounding fearful.

I stepped in front of him and squatted next to his left armpit. Eddie watched as I sniffed it.

"Phewww…" I said. "Your armpits sure do stink Eddie."

I placed a finger in his armpit and swirled it around, his sweat soaking my finger.

"You really enjoy cock teasing me don't you Eddie?" I asked him.

"I don't know what the hell you're talking about," Eddie replied.

I dug my fingertip deep into his armpit, tickling him.

"Ha, ha, ha!!!" Eddie laughed and squirmed helplessly on the bench.

I pulled on his armpit hairs.

"Admit it!" I said. "You're always cock teasing me."

"Okay, okay, I admit it!!" Eddie ranted. "I wanted you to see my body and drool over it. Now would you please stop tickling me and take the damned handcuffs off me???" I pulled my finger out of his hairy and sweaty armpit.

"I'll stop tickling you Eddie, for now," I said, looking intently into his eyes. "But I'm not going to un-cuff you for a while."

"WHY???" he asked me desperately.

"Because now you're going to get your wish," I replied with a grin. "I'm going to drool over your body."

I leaned down and began tonguing Eddie's left armpit, sniffing at it at the same time as I grabbed one of his nipples between my thumb and first finger. I squeezed and twisted his nipple as I worked his armpit with my tongue. Looking at me Eddie's eyes opened wide in shock.

"*Shit!!!*" he yelled shrilly. "Look at you eating at my disgusting armpit!!"

"I'm going to do the other one too," I quickly said.

I tongued Eddie's armpit deeply, swirling my tongue against his skin and thick hair in there. I even sucked some of his armpit hair into my mouth and slurped on it like it was a dick. I pulled his armpit hair hard with my lips, causing Eddie to cry out in a mixture of ecstasy and pain.

"SHIT!!!" he yelled. "This is how you thank me?"

"Thank you?" I asked him with a smile. "You wanted me to lust over you, you wanted me to see your hot body, and you wanted me to see you in your briefs!! Well now you're getting your wish."

"Yeah, and then some…" Eddie stated miserably as I went back to tonguing his left armpit.

The few hairs that wound up in my mouth I quickly spit on the floor. Eddie's sweat was delicious and I slurped it greedily into my mouth.

"You're a pervert Chris!" Eddie said to me. "I mean, whoever heard of someone sucking armpits???"

"Lots of people like it," I replied and quickly put my tongue back deep into his armpit.

With my thumb and first finger I continued twisting and squeezing one of Eddie's nipples. It was reacting just the way I had hoped it would. The nub was now erect and slowly swelling.

"OHHHHHHH fuck…" Eddie murmured.

I finally stopped working his left armpit and let go of Eddie's nipple. He breathed a loud sigh, almost as if he was disappointed that I'd stopped handling him. I stood up and looked down at him. He was totally helpless but not complaining at that point. Actually, in a way, Eddie seemed to be enjoying all of it. My dick throbbed long and hard in my briefs. I walked to the foot of the bench.

"Put your feet up and flat at the end of the bench," I said, lightly kicking Eddie's ankle.

Eddie did as he was told and I knelt down at his feet. I grabbed them in my hands at the ankles.

"What are you going to do now, lick my damned feet?" Eddie asked me.

"You got it," I said with a grin.

I leaned down and began running my tongue over the tops of Eddie's blue socked feet.

"Shit…" he said again. "I cannot believe this!!"

Eddie lifted his head up off the bench and watched as I licked the tops, sides, and bottoms of his feet. He didn't resist as I took one of his feet in both my hands and licked around his toes.

"Damn, I have to admit that that does feel great man," Eddie said breathlessly.

I noticed that the guy's dick was also hard in his white briefs. I continued lapping at his stinky toes under his sock. Eddie breathed in a man's passion. Then, I took his other foot in my hands and worked it the same way as I had the first one.

"Fuck, damned pervert is licking my stinking feet," Eddie grunted and laid his head back down on the bench.

By the time I was done Eddie's blue nylon dress socks were soaked with my saliva. I gave them a few last licks and then pulled his socks off his feet. The smell of Eddie's bare feet assaulted my nostrils. Actually, I could not wait to get started on Eddie's bare feet. They were at least size eleven.

"I'm going to keep these socks of yours as a souvenir when I'm done working you over Eddie," I said, holding up Eddie's smelly socks.

"Fuck man, you can have my damned socks!!" Eddie ranted. "Just let me up already!!"

I put Eddie's socks down on the floor and leaned my face over his bare stinking feet.

"Oh God, here we fucking go again…" Eddie said.

I took one of his big toes into my mouth and began sucking on it, long and hard.

"Oh shit, shit…" Eddie moaned in passion. "That feels so fucking good. Damn, my girlfriend never sucks my toes."

I slurped Eddie's big toe like crazy. After all the time we had been working together and me being secretly attracted to him my dream was coming true. Eddie was in my power and helpless to stop me from worshipping whatever part of his body I chose to. I stopped sucking his big toe and took it out of my mouth. I quickly replaced it with the next two toes on the foot I was presently working on. Eddie reeled in loud passion as I sucked two of his smelly toes at the same time.

"Oh yeah, you bastard…suck my damned toes…" Eddie panted.

I think Eddie was realizing at this point that *he was* enjoying what I was doing to him. When I was done sucking his toes I ran my tongue all over his bare feet, bathing them in my saliva. I paid special attention to the meaty bottoms of Eddie's beautiful feet. When I was done I wiped his feet dry with his socks and then slowly and ceremoniously rolled his blue dress socks onto his big feet and up to his calves. I folded down the tops of them like he had done earlier. I licked his socked feet a few times and then stood up. Slowly, I walked to the side of the bench and squatted down at Eddie's right armpit.

"Now, it's time to work on this other smelly pit of yours," I said to him, smiling lustfully.

Eddie didn't utter a single protest as I leaned my face down to his right armpit and began tonguing it. He breathed heavily and panted as my tongue swirled around heavily into his pit. Like with his other armpit I sucked on the thick hair, soaking it with my saliva. I took his swollen nipple between my thumb and first finger and began squeezing and twisting it. Eddie clenched his teeth in pain and pleasure at the same time. His dick and mine were throbbing in our briefs. Later for them though I thought. I still had more on my mind where Eddie's pits and tits were concerned. I was far from done…

When I was finished slurping, licking and sucking Eddie's right armpit I stood up, letting go of his nipple again. By now that nipple was more than erect and swollen. It looked ready to be sucked like crazy. And suck it I would, soon…

"You going to let me up now?" Eddie asked me.

"Yes I am," I replied, a fiendish smile on my face.

"Oh no, what are you up to now?" Eddie asked.

I got the key for the handcuffs from the other pocket of my suit pants and only unlocked the cuff around the weight bar. Eddie sat up, looking at me helplessly.

"I should kick your ass for this!!" he seethed.

"Later for that Eddie," I said, grabbing his cuffed wrists and pulling him to his feet. "Right now I want to have some more fun with that hot body of yours." I walked Eddie over to the chin-up bar, pulled his arms up above him, and locked the cuff around the chin-up bar. Eddie stood suspended from the bar, practically on his toes, but with enough slack so as not to hurt his wrists or cut off his blood circulation.

"UHHHnnn…" he moaned. "This isn't too comfortable…"

Ignoring him I left the room.

"Hey!!" Eddie yelled out to me. "Wh-where the hell are you going man? Don't leave me like this!!"

I returned less than two minutes later with a large bottle of cold mineral water that I had found in Eddie's refrigerator.

"I'm going to cool you down a little," I said, stepping in front of him. "Then I'm going to work on you some more…"

Eddie watched as I uncapped the bottle of water. I put it to his lips and gave him a few generous gulps of the stuff. He swallowed it greedily.

"Damn, I didn't realize how thirsty I was," Eddie said to me.

Then, I poured some water into my hand and rubbed the cool liquid over Eddie's rock hard chest, paying special attention to his nipples.

"Ohhhhh man, that feels good…" Eddie said breathlessly as he leaned his head back and stood on his toes.

Next, I poured more water into my hand and rubbed it into his armpits, thoroughly soaking them. I gave them a few licks and then rubbed more mineral water into them. Then, I leaned down a little and placed my lips near Eddie's erect, swollen nipple.

"Now tell me my friend, does your girlfriend ever do this for you?" I asked him and took the nipple into my mouth.

I began sucking, bighting and slurping on it like crazy.

"OHHHHHHHHH GOD!!!" Eddie roared and looked down at me. "OHHHHHH fuckin' shit man!! Y-you're sucking my damned fucking titty!!!"

Eddie squirmed in his bondage and reeled in the forced ecstasy as I worked his nipple. With my free hand I teased his other nipple with my thumb and fingers.

"Goddamn…" Eddie panted breathlessly.

When I was done working Eddie's nipples I looked longingly at his briefs, holding the bottle of mineral water at the ready in my hand.

"WH-what now???" Eddie asked me. "Please man, work my tits some more…just a little…*please man, please…*"

Eddie leaned forward and we kissed on the lips.

"You're gay aren't you?" I asked him. "You don't have a girlfriend…"

"I-I always thought so…but I think I'm sure now…" Eddie responded.

I kissed him again. His tongue explored my mouth. Then, I soaked his briefs with mineral water and knelt down in front of him.

"Start chinning," I said. "And don't stop till I tell you to."

Eddie jumped and grabbed the chin-up bar. He crossed his legs behind him, started chinning, and I started licking his sweat and water soaked briefs, running my tongue over his hard dick through the thin white cotton material. It tasted delicious, to say the least. I ran my hands over Eddie's strong muscular legs, his sexy thighs, and continued slurping on his briefs. Slowly, he became exhausted as he chinned more and more. Finally, I told Eddie to stop chinning. He stood back down, practically on his toes and looked at me beseechingly.

"M-my arms hurt so bad man…please…please let me down…" he begged.

I can't tell you how hot he looked. A black muscular man in bondage wearing white soaked briefs. Think about it and see if it doesn't give you a raging hard-on. Eddie's dick was hard and throbbing in his briefs. I could not wait anymore to get my lips wrapped around it and milk it.

"I'll let you down man, after one more thing…" I said and placed my hands on the sides of his soaked briefs.

Slowly, I pulled Eddie's briefs down and off him. I knelt in front of his dick, looking at it in awe. It was long, fat and oozing droplets of pre cum from the wide sexy piss slit. Eddie's big balls hung down low in his sac.

"What a fucking piece of meat…" I whispered, sniffing Eddie's sweaty balls.

They tingled in his sac.

"Oh God oh God," Eddie panted as I opened my mouth wide and slowly took his dick into it, lips first. "OH fuck, oh my fucking God!!!"

I sucked Eddie's meat slowly at first, paying attention to the crown of it with my lips, drooling on it and slurping my drool back into my mouth. I salivated like crazy all over it and swallowed Eddie's delicious pre-cum.

"What a fucking workout this turned out to be…" Eddie said, looking down at me.

I took more and more of his huge dick into my mouth with each suck till I finally managed to take the entire piece of giant tube steak into my throat. Eddie crooned in ecstasy as I deep throated his cock and took his balls in my fingers. His pubic hair was pressed against my face. Slowly, I took his giant piece of meat out of my throat and held it gently in my mouth, running my tongue over it, swirling it like it was an ice-cream cone.

"OH God…" Eddie said shrilly. "My damn arms are numb now…"

I sucked Eddie's meat a little faster now, tugging on his balls. I tickled his piss hole with the tip of my tongue.

"OHHHHH…getting there now…" Eddie announced.

Suddenly, he shot a load big enough to choke a goat. I swallowed the big spurts of his juices and even let some of it drip down my chin and onto my chest. Eddie reeled and screamed in ecstasy as I forced every possible drop of spunk out of his dick hole.

"OHHHHH fuck man, yeah!!!" Eddie ranted.

After he couldn't shoot any more juices I sucked his dick a little more, driving Eddie into a total frenzy. When I was done I unlocked the handcuff holding Eddie to the chin-up bar but left his wrists cuffed in front of him. He was still shaking in ecstasy as I helped him over to the weight bench. He sat down and I massaged his muscular arms to get the blood flowing properly in them.

"Feeling okay?" I asked him.

Eddie looked at me and smiled in exhaustion.

"I cannot begin to tell you how I'm feeling…" he replied and kissed me on the lips.

Then, Eddie asked me to stand up in front of him. Seeing as he had been pretty cooperative throughout his ordeal I did as he requested. With his hands still cuffed in front of himself he knelt down in front of me. Slowly, Eddie slid my underpants off me.

"May I suck your dick?" he asked me.

Without replying I placed my hand on the back of Eddie's head and guided him forward. Before taking me in his mouth he sniffed my dick a few times. Then, as he sucked me slowly and gingerly Eddie ran his cuffed hands over my legs and calves, toying with my black socks. When I was about to shoot my load I pulled my dick out of Eddie's mouth, told him to hold his arms above himself, and shot my pent-up load onto his magnificent chest, his nipples, and even into his luscious armpits.

Moments later Eddie was laying on the weight bench again, his hands cuffed to the weight bar again. He watched as I slurped my cum out of his armpits, off his chest, and off his nipples, torturing them at the same time.

"When are you going to un-cuff me man?" Eddie asked desperately.

I smiled at him and told him it was going to be a long night, adding that it would be a while before I had gotten enough of playing with a body like his. I slapped Eddie's chest and pulled one of his nipples back into my mouth.

"Looks like we'll both be calling in sick to work tomorrow…" Eddie murmured.

HORROR CAMP

By Christopher Trevor

"Man, I can't believe this is happening!!" I roared angrily at the man in the driver's seat of the car that I was literally trapped in. "Fucker, kidnapped me man, that's what you've done, fucking kidnapped me! And no matter what or who you are this is illegal shit!! You can't just come to a guy's apartment and snag him out of it like you did to me!"

I shot him an angry look from the passenger seat that I was tied to at the wrists down at my sides. He simply ignored me and continued calmly driving through the quiet night on the very deserted road that we were on.

"Fuck man, *this is really messed up and shitty!!"* I went on in angry tone of voice through clenched teeth. "I mean, how can you even think that I had an affair with your wife? Shit, she's not even my type!!"

Suddenly, he braked the car to a screeching halt. I was glad he had seat-belted me in otherwise I would have gone flying through the windshield. He turned to face me, grabbed a handful of my neck length dark brown hair and savagely yanked my head back till it was resting on the headrest of the passenger seat.

"Acccchhhhh!!!" I screeched.

"If you don't shut the fuck up from here on handsome boy I'm goin' to gag you, you slimy bastard," he said meanly, his teeth clenched and his face directly over mine, close enough to fucking kiss me actually. "And the only thing I can think of using to gag you with is one of my stinking and rancid socks!! I don't want to have to listen to your stupid prattle all the way to where I'm taking you! *Now, is all that clear and totally understood, Romeo?*"

"Y-yeah," I gasped breathlessly.

He let go of my hair, settled back in the driver's seat and I slowly moved my head facing forward. He restarted the car and calmly continued driving as I caught my breath. As we moved deeper and deeper into a very rural area of upstate New York my heart pounded in a mixture of fear and anger. I licked my dried and trembling lips and looked out the window at the miles and miles of woods on both sides of us. *Where the fuck was he taking me? What did he have in mind for me? And why the fuck hadn't Linda shown up just a tad earlier?* If she had I wouldn't be tied up in the passenger seat of my boss' husband's car heading for an unknown destination. Actually, if he hadn't snagged me that Saturday night I was sure that I would have eventually been taking this unplanned trip with him. As I went on looking out the window my thoughts returned to when Sam Michaels had abducted me, right out of my own fucking apartment no less…

It was a Saturday night and I had a date with a girl named Linda who I had met in a yuppie bar after work on Wednesday night. When I called her on Thursday morning and asked her to go out that Saturday she instantly accepted. Sam Michaels was right in calling me Romeo that was for sure bud. I asked Linda where I should pick her up and she surprised the fuck out of me by replying that she would pick *me* up at *my place*, in her car. At first I didn't like that idea, being the macho fuck that I am, but then I realized that she was a real woman of the twenty-first century. And if I wanted to get in her panties I would have to play it her way. So I agreed to have her pick me up at my place at eight o'clock on Saturday night. After hanging up the phone I leaned back in my office chair, placed my hands behind my head and propped my size eleven feet up on my desk.

"Life is good," I muttered, thinking of Saturday night and when I thought about what I would be doing with Linda I felt a pleasant stirring in my suit pants.

When Saturday night rolled around I showered at seven PM and shaved. As I stood there in the shower with the warm water cascading over my muscular body my big dick pointed straight up, long, hard and fat, dribbling beads of pre cum and throbbing like crazy, throbbing as I thought of Linda. She truly was one of the most beautiful women I had met in a long time. When I was done I stepped out of the shower stall and stood in front of the full-length mirror in the bathroom. I wiped the mist off the mirror and looked at my reflection. I'm exactly six feet tall, I have wavy dark brown hair, dark brown chestnut shaped eyes and I am extremely muscular and well toned from the workouts and swim laps that I put myself through at the gym on a daily basis every night after work. I'm two months away from my thirtieth birthday. Smiling at my reflection I ran my big hands over my muscular, somewhat hairy and rock hard chest and moved one hand down to my still rock hard dick. I hefted my big juicy and bulging balls in my hand and whispered one word, "Linda." I walked to my bedroom to get dressed for my date. Dinner, a movie and then her place I figured as I pulled on a pair of black knee length ribbed dress socks. I dressed in a dark blue suit, a white shirt, a red silk tie and black cap-toe shoes. I checked my reflection in the bedroom mirror and was more than satisfied with how I looked. I glanced at the clock on my night table; it was seven forty five. She would be arriving within fifteen minutes. As I looked back at my reflection a second time the doorbell rang. She was early I thought. I quickly turned off the bedroom light and dashed to the door of the apartment.

"A little early aren't you baby?" I asked as I opened the door and suddenly realized that it had been the doorbell outside my apartment that had rung and not the buzzer from the lobby. "I-uh, who are you?"

I stood there with my apartment door wide open, looking at a tall and burly looking guy who I had never seen before, but for whatever the reason he looked strangely familiar. He was wearing a plaid cotton button down shirt with worn looking blue jeans and tan work boots.

"Mr. John Giglo?" he asked me, looking at me with a slight smirk on his face.

"That's me, what can I do for you?" I asked in reply.

Suddenly and without any warning he raised his big hands, pressed them firmly against my chest and shoved me with great force backward into my apartment.

"Uhhhnnnffff!!!" I gasped, startled.

I fell backward, but managed to stay on my feet, landing against a wall. The guy stepped into the apartment slammed the door behind him and walked toward me, a fierce look of angry determination etched on his face.

"Wh-what is this?" I stammered. *"Wh-who the fuck are you?"*

He grabbed me by my jacket lapels, pulled me away from the wall, practically hoisted me off my damned feet and shoved me hard again. This time I did fall, backward and stumbling over my coffee table, landing in a heap in front of my couch.

"Hey now, hold on here Mister!!" I yelled angrily, looking up at him from the floor. *"Just what the fuck is going on here???"*

In reply he grabbed me from behind by my belt, hauled me roughly to my feet and swung me around the room.

"Uhhhhhnnnnnn!!!" I gasped, my arms flailing helplessly out in front of me. "H-hey!! C-c'mon man, take it easy huh?"

He did what I dreaded he was going to do. He let go of my belt, sending me spiraling uncontrollably across the room. I knocked over a lamp and slammed bodily hard into a wall, sliding to the floor, absolutely stunned.

"What're you all dolled up for Giglo?" he asked me mockingly, slowly stepping over to where I had landed. "Got a hot date with another victim tonight maybe?"

I looked up at him in total confusion and he kicked my outstretched thigh.

"OWWWW!!" I howled in pain.

"Get on your feet you bastard!" he said meanly through clenched teeth.

Trying to make some sort of sense of what was happening I slowly began to stand up. The guy tripped me, sending me back to the floor. I landed hard this time on my ass.

"Ufffff!!!" I sputtered. "Fucker."

"Bastard, I should kill you man!!" the guy roared, leaned down, grabbed me by my necktie and hauled me to my wobbly feet. "You fucking shit!! Look at you, all dolled up and raring to go like a damned Romeo or something!!"

He swung me around again, holding me tightly by my tie, looking into my eyes gleefully as he spun me and spun me.

"Pl-please man," I panted, clawing my hands around the upper part of my tie.

When he let go I was slammed hard against another wall.

"Ohhhhrrr shit," I gasped.

Then, holding my tie like a leash he forced me over to the couch and sat me down hard. I placed my hands on the sides of my poor throbbing head, looking helplessly down at the floor. The fucker had taken me by surprise and knocked the wind right the fuck out of me. I was sure at that moment that I was going to be robbed and probably killed, and just before one of the hottest dates of my life. Linda would find me dead in my apartment I thought miserably.

"Who are you?" I asked him again.

"Michaels," the man replied, placing his booted foot on my coffee table and looking down at me scornfully. "Does that name mean anything to you Johnny boy?"

Before I could reply he grabbed my chin and turned my head so that I was looking up at him.

"M-Michaels, that's my boss' last name," I choked through trembling lips.

"I'm her husband, Sam Michaels," he seethed, his lips so close to mine that I thought for sure he was going to kiss me.

"Wh-why're you here, doin' this to me?" I asked him and my trembling lips grazed his.

His lips tasted of cigar tobacco.

"You have some set of balls on you to be asking me that question Romeo," he replied, letting go of my chin, but still looming menacingly over me. "You think I don't know what you and my wife have been doing?"

I looked at him in utter confusion. What the hell was he talking about? And then I realized why he had looked familiar to me. My boss, his wife had a picture of him and her on her desk at the office.

"What are you talking about?" I asked him, a look of utter incomprehension on my face.

"You've been fucking her Mr. Giglo!!" he spat at me. "Right in my home too!"

With that he again grabbed me by my lapels, hauled me meanly off the couch and flung me over the coffee table. I landed on the floor on my stomach. Fucking guy was strong and quick that was for sure.

"Ohhhhrrr," I moaned in pain as he yanked me up to my feet.

I tried to make a fist and pummel the bastard, but he was too fast for me. He delivered two hard, full packed punches to my stomach, I doubled over in pain, my arms crossed protectively over my mid section, gasping, trying desperately to catch my breath, trying to make some sense of what was happening here. But overall I realized I was in a shit-load of trouble at the moment.

"I-I honestly don't know what you're talking about," I said slowly, my stomach still aching from the two punches he had delivered to it.

"I didn't expect you to admit it Johnny boy, but maybe after we get to where I'm taking you your memory will return," he said to me.

Slowly and cautiously I uncrossed my arms from in front of my stomach and looked at him in disbelief.

"T-taking me?" I asked him, thoroughly confused and very frightened now. "Wh-what does that mean?"

"It means Romeo that you and I are going for a ride, *a long ride*," he said, stepping quickly behind me and grabbing my arms, yanking them up painfully behind my back. "And we're going to be spending all of tomorrow together."

"Owwwww!!!" I bellowed as he twisted my arms. "Wh-where the fuck are you planning on taking me man?"

"My wife and I own a children's camp in a remote, very out of the way area in upstate New York," he said, holding my arms tightly behind me. "It's closed at the moment so it's the perfect place for you and me to go and spend some quality time together, where I can teach you a lesson for fucking my wife. Now, let's get going. We are leaving this instant."

"Man, what the fuck do I have to do to convince you that I did not fuck Mrs. Michaels???" I asked him desperately as he started moving me toward the door, his crotch rubbing erotically against my rear end. "Look man, I have a date tonight with a real foxy lady and…"

"And your date has just been canceled Mr. Giglo," he said harshly and yanked on my arms real hard, causing a searing pain to rip through me. "Now listen and listen closely stud boy, we're going down in the elevator, if you do anything to try to get away from me you will pay dearly. You've already had a dose of what I'm capable of."

To add even more credibility to what he had just said he yanked hard on my arms again and forced me to double over in pain.

"Ohhhhrrrrr!!!" I moaned miserably.

Then, I felt the cold steel of a handcuff close around one of my wrists.

"Goddamn it," I mumbled.

Mr. Michaels found one of my overcoats in my closet and draped it over my shoulders, effectively hiding the fact that my hands were cuffed behind me.

"It is so hot out that if anyone sees me with this overcoat on they'll think it strange," I said to him, trying not to let my fear show.

"So?" he asked me, straightening out my askew necktie. "Stranger things are seen everyday here in New York City."

When we exited my apartment it was eight PM on the dot. Linda had just missed seeing me being abducted, right out of my own damned apartment. In the elevator Mr. Michaels pressed the button marked "G" and we descended toward the garage. We rode all the way down in silence. The elevator didn't stop once to pick up any passengers, to my utter and total dismay. In the garage Mr. Michaels quickly hustled me over to his car and deposited me in the passenger seat. Once I was seated he gave me two hard punches to my stomach.

"Arrrrghhhh, geez," I gasped and doubled over again in pain.

As I sat there helplessly in pain he quickly took the handcuffs off me and got my hands roped at the wrists to the sides of the seat. The way he had my hands roped anyone who might look into the car would not be able to see that I was tied to the seat. Lastly he seat belted me in.

"A warning," he said as he settled into the driver's seat and pressed the tip of a finger against the side of my face. "If you try to summon any help at the toll booths along the way I'll make you very sorry, so fucking sorry that your pea brain can't even conceive of it. Got that Romeo?"

I nodded glumly and he moved the tip of his finger over my trembling lips.

"God you're a handsome fuck," he said meanly and started the car.

As we pulled out of the garage I saw Linda getting out of her car in front of the apartment building. I choked back tears.

After Mr. Michaels had threatened to gag me with one of his socks I stayed silent for the next half-hour or so of the ride. But I needed to have one very important question answered. I cleared my throat and decided to take a chance in speaking to him.

"Er-Mr. Michaels, Sir, may I ask you a question?" I said very softly.

"Go ahead," he replied, keeping his eyes on the dark road ahead of us.

"Why do you think I had an affair with your wife?" I asked him.

He pursed his lips together in an angry looking grimace and then seemed to relax. Keeping one hand on the wheel he reached into the breast pocket of his cotton plaid shirt.

"Does this look familiar to you?" he asked, holding up a white, men's handkerchief.

On the side of the handkerchief I saw the monogrammed initials "JG", my initials.

"It's mine," I whispered. "Or at least it was; I gave it to your wife."

"I found it in between the sheets, *on our bed,*" he said angrily, crumpled the handkerchief into a ball and threw it at me.

It hit me in the face and landed in my lap.

"You think that because you found my handkerchief in your bed sheets that I'm having an affair with your wife?" I asked him in disbelief.

"Enough talk Mr. Giglo," he said and slammed on the breaks.

"Oh no, no," I muttered as he unlaced one of his big work boots.

I watched helplessly as he pulled his foot out of his right boot and pulled his white sweat sock off, inside out. The rancid scent of his boot, foot and sock wafted up at me. He balled the sock up and leaned toward me. I was totally unable to resist as he crammed the foul stinking thing into my mouth, his other hand holding tightly to the back of my neck.

"We ain't goin' to see anybody along this road so no one will see that I have a bound and now gagged passenger in my car," Mr. Michaels said, tying a length of rope over the sock in my mouth, which he had gotten out of the glove compartment.

Then, he slipped his work boot onto his bare foot and started the car again. I sat there in total despair as we drove on, but I was totally shocked when I realized that my dick was hard as a fucking rock in my suit pants. Mr. Michaels wasn't kidding when he said that his socks were rancid, they were worse than that. The taste of his feet sweat assaulted my taste buds and slid down my throat.

"MMMfffff," I sputtered angrily and my dick pounded long and hard in my pants.

We arrived at the camp about two hours or so later. (By my best estimates that is.) I saw a sign with a florescent light over it which read "Welcome to Camp Michaels." At the bottom of the sign was a painted drawing of a smiling face. I felt like anything but smiling at that moment.

"We're here," Mr. Michaels said fiendishly as he parked the car in front of a big cabin.

Looking out the window of the car I saw various cabins, a set of monkey bars, two sliding ponds, a few seesaws, and two rows of swings and in the distance what looked like a kiddy pool. Woods, miles upon miles of woods surrounded the campgrounds. Being a city boy at heart I felt totally out of my element in this place. Mr. Michaels stopped the car and looked at me, almost lustfully.

"God, you look real miserable with my damned sock crammed in that pretty mouth of yours stud boy, you ready for a not so pleasant stay here at camp Michaels?" he guffawed.

He gingerly undid the rope around the sock in my mouth.

"Not a damned word after I un-gag you Romeo," he said harshly. "You are not to speak unless I say so."

Then, he took his sock out of my mouth, used it to wipe my stray saliva off my lips and threw it down in my lap along with my monogrammed handkerchief. The scent of his sock stayed on my lips and in my mouth even after he had taken it out. I shivered in total fear as he withdrew a long hunting knife from under his seat. He leaned in close to me and ran the tip of the knife against my cheek, lovingly caressing my face with it.

"You do as I tell you and you'll be heading home tomorrow night by this time," he said to me breathlessly. "Disobey what I tell you and you'll pay severe consequences."

He ran the knife tip over the back of my neck and twirled a lock of my hair around one of his fingers.

"Do you understand all that Mr. Giglo?" he asked me and pressed the blade of the knife against the lock of my hair that he was holding.

I slowly nodded that I understood sweat pouring off me everywhere, my suit soaked in it. I was shaking uncontrollably, I was sniveling and choking back tears and I thought I was literally going to shit in my pants.

"Good man," Mr. Michaels said and sheered off the short lock of my hair that he was holding with the hunting knife.

"Ahhhhyyyy!!!" I cried as I felt the lock of my hair cut out at the root.

"Do as I say and you'll be fine," he told me again, holding up the lock of my hair for me to see.

"O-okay," I whispered, not able to hold back the tears now.

"Let's get out of the car," he said and slid the knife into one of his big boots.

Moments later I was standing next to the car massaging my numbed rope burned wrists. The air was thick with humidity and there wasn't even a breeze. I loosened my tie and undid the top button of my shirt. Mr. Michaels stood a few feet away from me, looking me over, seeming to drink in the sight of me.

"So, here we are you bastard," he said. "Just you and I and nature, and you are going to find Mr. Giglo that nature can be very cruel, very fucking cruel indeed. Now, get out of that fancy suit and tie that you're wearing. Ain't nobody up here to be all dolled up for."

I looked at him in disbelief.

"You can keep your shoes and socks on, but the rest goes," he said looking totally maniacally crazy at that point. "Get started, **now!!!**"

At the sound of his horribly loud yell birds flew out of trees in all directions. With my hands shaking I shucked off my suit jacket and tossed it in the open window of the car. Next, I took off my tie followed by my shirt.

"Doing a little strip tease for me eh you handsome fuck?" Mr. Michaels asked me mockingly as I tossed my shirt and tie in the car. "Bet my wife loved watching you strip for her."

He was looking in awe at my big muscular chest as I undid my suit pants. Moments later I was standing next to the car wearing just my black cap-toe shoes and knee length black nylon ribbed socks. My hands were over my crotch, hiding the big hard-on I was sporting. The fucking guy hadn't even allowed me to keep my damned briefs on.

"Get your hands away from your dick and balls and behind your head Romeo," Mr. Michaels said, approaching me. "A fucking macho stud like you should be more than proud of his manhood."

I did as he said, crossing my hands up behind my head. As sweat dripped off me more heavily big flies and hungry mosquitoes began finding their way to me, landing on my chest. When I tried to shoo them away Mr. Michaels again told me to get my hands above my head. I did as he said again because I thought he was going for the knife as he said it.

"See, I told you that Nature could be very cruel," he said, running the tip of a finger over my big chest. "Flies and mosquitoes are just two of the very, very pesky insects out here. After a while it can become torture while they're crawling all over you, biting you, making you itch like crazy. I'm sure glad I'll be spending the night in the manager's cabin with the air conditioner on high. But you won't be as fortunate Mr. Giglo. You will be spending the night out here, hooked up over there."

When he pointed his finger I looked in the direction he was indicating. Standing there all sexy in just my shoes and socks with my hands up over my head I let out a loud gulp. Mr. Michaels was pointing at the monkey bars and with his other hand he grabbed my hard dick.

"Come on Romeo, let's get some rope out of the truck of the car," Mr. Michaels said, looking at me fiendishly, holding and stroking my big hard-on as he moved me toward the car.

I was breathless...

Then, a little while later I found myself tightly and very securely roped to the sides of the metal monkey bars. I was in a spread eagle position, miserably stretched out like a big letter X, and tied with mounds upon mounds of rope at the wrists, ankles, my upper thighs and arms and around and around my chest and stomach areas. I looked down at the ground in anguish as Mr. Michaels looked up at me with total satisfaction. I appeared as if crucified.

"Now, maybe you'll sleep a little out here, but I truly doubt it Mr. Giglo," he said mockingly. "But if you don't sleep that's good for what I have in mind, because by morning you'll already be sapped and you have a long, hot and hard day ahead of you."

I squirmed miserably on the monkey bars as more flies and mosquitoes landed on my chest, my stomach, in my armpits and even on my dick and balls. When a big fly walked over one of my big nipples I let out a deep breath. I didn't utter another sound though for fear of Mr. Michaels' wrath.

"The way you're tied there's no danger of your blood circulation being cut off Mr. Giglo," he went on, running the palm of his hand over one of my highly shined shoes. "But by tomorrow morning when I untie you your limbs will be feeling more than awful, that much I can assure you of. Well, have a good night and I'll see you in the morning."

He smiled up at me, snapped the elastic in one of my socks against my leg and walked off toward the manager's cabin. I wanted to scream obscenities at him I wanted to kill him, the fucking bastard that he was. Shit, I was going to suffer horribly. When he went into the manager's cabin I saw the lights come on inside and then I heard the hum of the air conditioner as it came to life. I looked down at my bound muscular body in the moonlight and saw that more flies and mosquitoes had found their way to me. They were crawling up and down my legs, across my arms, over the back and front of my big neck and I could even feel them moving over my ass cheeks. To put it bluntly I was in a really fucked up situation… As I hung there my bound body glistened in the moonlight…

Somehow I must have dozed off for a while because when I opened my eyes I recalled having dreamt of Linda, her arms around me, kissing me tenderly on the lips, holding me close. My arms and legs were completely numb by now and the insects were feasting on me. I could actually feel them taking microscopic bites out of me. I was itching miserably. I looked at the manager's cabin, saw that all the lights were out and still heard the hum of the damned air conditioner. Fucking bastard was sleeping comfortably while I was roped up to those damned monkey bars, hanging there like a damned side of beef in a butcher's freezer. Except this was no freezer because it had to be at least ninety-five degrees with the humidity index at more than a hundred fucking percent. I was literally sopped in sweat by then. When I felt something big moving over one of my socked calves I looked down and nearly let out a loud scream. I clamped my mouth down on my lower lips and watched horrified as a medium sized lizard made its way stealthily up my leg. Its tongue flicked over my sock and it seemed to be looking hungrily at my low hanging nut sac.

"*Oh God,*" I squeaked.

I was able to move the portion of my leg that the lizard was crawling up and it lost its footing and fell to the ground. I breathed a sigh of relief as the thing scampered off.

When I opened my eyes again the seething sun was shining down on me, strong and intensely hot. I felt like I was being roasted.

"Ahhhhhrrrr," I groaned miserably as I came to and felt the rope around one of my feet being undone.

I looked down and as my vision cleared I saw Mr. Michaels untying the rope. He was dressed in worn looking denim shorts, a white tank top, his tan work boots and white sweat socks. The hunting knife was in his right boot, the handle of it sticking out, mocking me reminding me of who was in charge here. His body was as muscular as I thought it was. For whatever the reason my dick twitched and grew hard as I watched him untying my foot, his hand roaming over my sock every few seconds. On the ground next to him I saw a dog dish filled with scrambled eggs and bacon. On the side of that dog dish was another, filled with what looked like piss.

"Good morning you bastard," Mr. Michaels said, looking up at me mockingly. "I trust you had a pleasant evening."

I didn't reply, knowing that I still wasn't permitted the luxury of speaking. When I was completely untied and off the monkey bars I stood docile and still as Mr. Michaels stood behind me massaging life back into my numb arms. I stood there feeling stupid and real sexy at the same time, stripped to my shoes and socks, my dick hard as a rock and my nut sac hanging down real low and plump looking.

"As you can see breakfast is served asshole," he said to me, squeezing my upper arms. "I want you to eat up real fast because I have a hell of a day planned for you."

Then, it seemed as if the guy could read my mind because as I was contemplating fisting him good and hard he rapped me across the back of my head. He sent me to my knees, stunned. I gasped softly, my hand finding its way to the lump that was already forming on the back of my head.

"Start eating now shit head," he said sternly. "And make sure you drink up every drop of that piss of mine. Fuck, I worked hard to fill up that bowl for you during the night."

Trembling, I leaned over the dog dish filled with eggs and bacon and went to hand feed it to myself. Mr. Michaels kicked me hard across my naked buttocks.

"Not like that you asshole," he snarled down at me. "Eat like the dog you are."

Without looking up at him I did as he said and began eating like a dog, burying my face in the eggs and bacon. As I fed myself Mr. Michaels ran the tip of one of his boots against my ass crack. The tip of my dick was against the ground. It was hard and throbbing.

"You sure are one hell of a handsome dude Mr. Giglo," he said to me. "I can see why my wife and God knows how many other women would be so fucking anxious to have you fuck the shit out of them, but all that is over as of today. By the time I get done with you, you aren't going to be in any shape to fuck anyone for a long time to come."

I stopped eating for a moment and looked up at him in anguish, remnants of the bacon and eggs all over my face.

"Hurry up and chow down you asshole!" he yelled at me and gave my ass a hard swift kick.

"Uffff," I sputtered and buried my face back in the food.

When I was done eating the eggs and bacon I looked at the other dog dish in outright horror.

"Drink it you ass hole!!" Mr. Michaels snarled with authority. "You must be thirsty as hell by now, and it's the only fucking thing I'm going to let you drink all day!!"

I closed my eyes, leaned over the piss filled dog dish and stuck out my tongue. It smelled vile and rancid. I lapped up the piss as fast as I could. It was warm and tasted awful. When I was done I pulled myself to my knees and looked up at Mr. Michaels. Tears were streaming down my handsome face through the bits and pieces of egg and bacon on me.

"Crying already you big stupid lug?" he asked me and ruffled my hair. "Geez, by later on you're going to be fucking sobbing, *get on your feet ass hole!!"*

I pulled myself to my feet as Mr. Michaels picked up a backpack that had been on the ground behind him. He slung the backpack over his shoulder, took me by one arm and walked me into the woods. My dick was long and hard, pointing straight up to heaven. Within five minutes we came upon a large fallen tree branch.

"Ah, just what I was looking for," Mr. Michaels said. "Pick up that tree branch and sling it across those big strong shoulders of yours Giglo. We're going to see just how strong a guy you are."

As I squatted and picked up the heavy tree branch Mr. Michaels opened his backpack and pulled out some rope. In moments my wrists were securely tied to the ends of the tree branch which was slung across my shoulders. The rough bark bit into my skin and the weight of the damn thing was enormous on my shoulders. Mr. Michaels hung his backpack on the end of the tree branch and ordered me to get moving. With the heavy branch lashed meanly to my shoulders I began walking ahead of my captor. As I walked slowly and miserably in the seething heat Mr. Michaels threw pebbles and large rocks against my ass cheeks.

"Owwwwwwwrrrr!!!" I roared.

"Move it Romeo!!" Mr. Michaels shouted behind me. "We're just getting started on our nature hike!"

His backpack swung back and forth on the end of the tree branch as I plodded on in agony. A few times I stepped in mud puddles, getting my shoes filthy. As we walked through thorn bushes I was pinched on all parts of my exposed naked body. Mr. Michaels made sure to avoid all the thorn bushes and mud puddles. Sweat dripped off me everywhere and more and more insects were finding their way to me.

"RRRRR!!!!" I roared through clenched teeth as flies landed on my face and crawled on it, making me itch like crazy.

As I walked Mr. Michaels took a riding crop out of his backpack and whacked my ass hard with it. "Arrrgghhhh!!!" I cried loudly and could feel my sexy ass cheeks jiggling madly as he rapped them again with the damned riding crop. "Ayyyyyrrrrrr!!!!"

"Walk faster," Mr. Michaels said and whacked my ass again and again to get me moving faster and faster.

I quickly discovered how difficult it is to walk through the woods in a pair of cap-toe shoes. Having a tree branch lashed to your shoulders and having your ass cheeks whipped makes it even more difficult. GOD!!! After we had been walking for about a half-hour or so Mr. Michaels told me to stop. I did as he said and turned to face him. My dick was pointing straight out, long, hard and fat.

"Man, you look awful," he said and slapped one of my big muscular pecs good and hard.

"Uhhhh," I moaned miserably and tottered on my shaky feet.

"Kneel down Giglo," he said to me threateningly.

I took a deep breath and slowly slid to my knees in front of him. The dirt ground bit into my bare skin, irritating the fuck out of me. By now the tree branch felt like it weighed hundreds of pounds as it pressed down on my now aching and scratched up shoulders.

"Thirsty?" Mr. Michaels asked me.

I nodded that I was, looking up at him beseechingly. He unzipped his shorts and whipped his whopper of a dick out of them. He held his dick steady over my trembling lips and pissed. I gulped down as much of his piss as I could; I wanted to drink as much as possible. It tasted as awful as it had earlier, but I was in no position to complain. I was that thirsty bud. As I gulped down his piss I ran the tip of my tongue over the tip of his dick a few times. He didn't complain or make comment of it as I gulped down more of his yellow stream. When he was done pissing he packed his big whopper of a dick back into his shorts and looked at me sternly.

"Okay asshole, back on your feet!" Mr. Michaels said to me.

A look of utter defeat crossed over my face and I slowly pulled myself to my aching feet, the tree branch pressing down harder than ever on my shoulders. When I was standing Mr. Michaels looked me over. I was a six foot tall sweaty mess, my butt cheeks were striped red from the lashes he had given me with the riding crop, my shoulders and legs were aching and insects were crawling all over me. Yet my dick remained long and fucking hard. Yeah, Mr. Michaels was going to make super sure that I was more than beat to shit when this was over.

"I just came up with a great idea," Mr. Michaels said, looking wickedly at my plump juicy balls.

What now I thought miserably as Mr. Michaels took some more rope out of his backpack, which was still hanging on the end of the tree branch lashed across my poor shoulders. Mr. Michaels tied some rope tightly around my balls, just under the base of my hard dick. Then, he stepped behind me and told me to get moving again. As I walked he used the rope as a sort of leash to pull on my tied balls. He laughed as I walked like a dog on a leash. My balls were pulled under me and behind me and a few times I thought he was going to yank them right off me as he pulled on that damned rope. *What a fucked up situation I was in, and all because of a misunderstanding.* My dick pointed straight out, long and hard in front of me. I walked on, aching, sweating, gasping for breath and crying profusely. I didn't deserve this I thought miserably as I trudged on.

"Enjoying the walk so far asshole?" Mr. Michaels asked and yanked on the rope around my balls.

"Owwwww!!!" I cried out in reply.

Mr. Michaels laughed, pulled hard on the rope again and again I screamed in pain. As I plodded on and on I pissed a few times, my piss streaming down my legs, on my socks and on my shoes. I was surprised that the fucking guy didn't punish me for pissing without his permission. As I pissed I looked down at my feet. My expensive cap-toe shoes were covered in mud, dirt and filth and my black nylon dress socks were spotted with mud and dirt. Flies and other summer insects were crawling over my knees, my thighs and the backs of my thighs, making me itch more and more like crazy. I felt insects crawling over my ass cheeks and when I looked down again there was a bee crawling through the sweat all over my chest. It stopped on one of my nipples and I thought for sure that it was going to sting me. I clenched my teeth in readiness for the pain I was about to feel. But after sitting there on my nipple for a few minutes the bee flew off. I cried harder and harder in agony and at the injustice of what Mr. Michaels was doing to me. As my tears flowed down my cheeks I plodded on miserably, my poor balls aching and pulled under my ass crack. Then, at one awful point I felt what I was sure were big old horse flies crawling over my ass crack. I feared that they would find their way into my ass hole so I squeezed my butt cheeks together as tightly as possible as I plodded on. Mr. Michaels saw what I was doing and laughed hysterically and mockingly.

"I just love seeing you suffer Giglo," Mr. Michaels said jokingly and threw a few pebbles at my ass cheeks.

Even though it hurt like the devil I kept my ass cheeks squeezed tightly closed, still fearing that the flies that I felt crawling back there would somehow get inside my hole. *God!!!*

"Halt!!!" Mr. Michaels barked at me fifteen minutes or so later.

I stopped walking and did my best to stand in place as Mr. Michaels stepped in front of me. I was heaving for breath by then and he saw that. I was literally sopped in sweat from head to toe and shaking and trembling all over. A look of concern came into Mr. Michaels' eyes.

"Better get that branch off you now," he said. "I don't want you dropping dead on me after all. I only have you out here to teach you a much needed lesson."

Admittedly I was grateful as he untied my wrists from the branch, took his backpack off the end of it and pushed it off my shoulders. I lowered my aching arms to my sides and fell to my knees in front of the man who had kidnapped me. With my head hanging down I sobbed loud and miserably. I knelt there shaking, crying and pissing on the ground. I looked up at Mr. Michaels and quickly noticed that the look of concern I saw earlier was gone from his eyes.

"On your feet Giglo," he said, giving my balls a good hard yank, reminding me again of who was in charge.

I found myself a few minutes later tied with my wrists over me to a tree branch above me, my feet firmly on the ground. Mr. Michaels stepped behind me with the riding crop in hand. I didn't need three guesses to know what I was in for at that moment. He raised the riding crop high, swung it down and it connected horribly with my butt cheeks.

"Arrrrrhhhhh!!!" I cried as he whacked me a second and third time with the riding crop. "Ayyyrrrrr!!"

My balls were still tied and in between beating my butt cheeks Mr. Michaels would give them a good hard yank, getting a good shrill scream out of me each time. I clenched my teeth and balled my roped hands into fists in agony as Mr. Michaels pummeled my ass cheeks more and more, harder and harder with each blow.

"Urrrrrhhhh!!!!" I seethed as he savagely beat my ass cheeks, showing me no mercy whatsoever.

I bucked my muscular sexy body back and forth, dancing around stupidly as Mr. Michaels went on beating my ass, harder and harder still with each blow.

"Ohhhhrrrrr!!!" I whimpered breathlessly and felt the welts popping up on my ass cheeks.

Then, Mr. Michaels grabbed the rope around my balls, gave it a hard tug and it happened. *I couldn't believe it, but it fucking happened.* I shot my load of pent-up cum, right there in the middle of the woods, while hanging from a damned tree, *having my ass beaten with a riding crop I shot my damned load.*

"Ohhhhrrrrr!!!!" I cried out in a definite mixture of pain and pleasure.

"Well I'll be damned," Mr. Michaels said as my thick creamy cum landed on the ground in front of me. "Fucking came like gangbusters didn't you Romeo? Looks like all this shit I'm heaping on you is exciting you eh?"

I quickly nodded "no" as he swung the riding crop toward my ass cheeks and I shot another glob of sperm.

"Ayyyyyyyrrrrr!!!!" I screamed.

Seconds later he had me screaming in agony and in a lather all over again as he whipped the tar out of my ass with the riding crop over and over again.

"Ayyyyyyy!!!!" I screamed loud and pitifully as I danced and bucked around like crazy.

When Mr. Michaels finally stopped beating my ass cheeks with the riding crop he gave my balls a few last tugs with the rope and then untied my wrists from the tree branch. I ran my palms over my much wounded ass cheeks and felt the big welts back there. With my hands still pressed against my sexy wounded ass cheeks I looked at Mr. Michaels miserably, ready to defend my honor.

"Not a word just yet Mr. Giglo," he said, grabbing and squeezing one of my nipples, giving it a hard twist.

I screamed loudly in pain.

"I'm not yet ready to listen to anything you have to say," he said and twisted my nipple real hard again, squeezing the fuck out of it.

I saw stars and my head spun. A while later, with my hands now tied in front of me and the rope still tied around my poor aching balls I sat on a tree stump eating a plain bologna sandwich which Mr. Michaels had had in his backpack. He sat on the ground a few feet from where I was sitting, eating a sandwich also.

"I can't believe it's the early afternoon already," he said, looking at his watch. "And I still have plenty more nasty shit planned for you Giglo."

I rolled my eyes in disbelief as he handed me another sandwich.

"Eat up asshole," Mr. Michaels said as I took the sandwich from him. "You must be more than ravenous after the workout I just put you through."

I looked at him miserably and took a bite of the second sandwich. When I was done eating Mr. Michaels made me kneel down on the ground and tilt my head back so I could have a drink, of his piss. He held his flaccid dick over my open mouth and pissed a long yellow stream for me to quench my thirst with. His muscular body shivered in ecstasy when I ran the tip of my tongue over the tip of his dick. Neither of us made comment about it however. When I was done drinking his piss Mr. Michaels looked at me mockingly as he sipped cool water from his canteen.

"Time to get moving again Giglo," he said to me as he packed his dick into his shorts. "But first I want to get you ready for the next leg of this journey."

Minutes later my hands were securely tied behind me and I watched in tortured agony as Mr. Michaels took two clip-on clothespins out of his backpack. I took two steps backward, but it did no good at all. Mr. Michaels clipped the clothespins onto my nipples.

"Ayyyyrrrrr!!!!" I cried out loudly and he tugged hard on the rope *still* tied around my balls.

The clothespins bit and squeezed my poor fleshy nipples hard and unforgivingly.

"Okay asshole, let's get moving, now!!" Mr. Michaels barked at me.

With no other choice than to do as I was told I turned my back to him and began walking again. My nipples, to put it plainly felt awful and my balls were swollen at this point from having that damned rope tied around them for so long. I was more than a sweaty and stinking mess by now, the inside of my mouth tasted awful from being pissed in and the flies and mosquitoes were again feasting on me. As I walked slowly and miserably Mr. Michaels trotted up behind me and gave my ass cheeks a few hard whacks with the riding crop to get me moving quicker.

"Arrrrhhhh!!!!" I screamed, each time he whacked my poor ass cheeks.

My dick, for whatever damned reason was again hard as a fucking rock and throbbing like crazy in front of me. I knew that when Mr. Michaels tugged on that rope again I would definitely shoot another load of cream, GOD, what was happening to me??? The bastard kept on whacking my ass cheeks though, making me move faster and faster through the hot and humid woods. The clothespins on my nipples weighed the poor things down and my balls ached horribly…

An hour or so later we came upon a fallen tree. Mr. Michaels ordered me to halt and looked at the fallen tree in awe.

"Just what I was hoping to find," he murmured and looked at me fiendishly.

I hunched my shoulders up and looked at him miserably, knowing I was in for more nastiness as Mr. Michaels made me walk over to the fallen tree. He stretched me out on my muscular back on top of the fallen tree and proceeded to tie my feet firmly together. As I lay there with my hands roped behind me, my feet tied together, my balls still trussed the clothespins on my nipples and sweating like a pig Mr. Michaels loomed over me, the riding crop in his hand.

"You know I really should tie you down to that tree and leave you out here," he said to me, seeming to mean it. "By nightfall some damned animal would undoubtedly find you and make a meal out of you, but I can't do that and you know it you slimy bastard."

He grabbed the rope around my balls, tugged hard on it twice and I shot my second load.

"Arrrrrhhhhh!!!!" I groaned loudly and writhed in ecstasy on top of the fallen tree, the bark biting and scratching my skin and irritating the welts on my ass cheeks.

"Fucker that you are," Mr. Michaels said to me as my cum splashed onto my chest and stomach. "Loving all this shit, look at you cumming like a bitch in heat!"

He twisted my balls and squeezed them hard.

"Ayyyyyrrrr!!!" I screamed and lifted my upper body up off the tree as more ropes of sperm erupted from my slit.

Mr. Michaels grabbed the riding crop, pressed the tip of it against my chest and pushed me back down onto my back, stretching me back out on the tree. I cried loudly through clenched teeth, trembled atop that damned tree and snot dribbled out of my nose. God almighty I was a disaster. Mr. Michaels stepped to my side and raised the riding crop.

"Ohhhrrrrr!!!!" I roared in agony as he brought the riding crop down across my stomach. "Ohhhhrrrr!!!"

I bucked and squirmed and writhed on that fallen tree as Mr. Michaels proceeded to pummel my stomach area, sending shockwaves of pain through me. He rapped my chest area and my upper thighs as well with that damned riding crop. I screamed loudly in tortured agony and utter frustration as the man worked me over like crazy. When he was done a little while later there were red stripes all over my body. I lay there whimpering as he whipped out his dick and pissed liberally all over my chest and stomach.

"Bastard, you don't even deserve to drink my damned piss at this point!!" he yelled at me as he moved down and pissed over my socks. "Fucking home wrecker."

That did it; I lifted my upper body up off the tree and looked at him in total anger, fire seeming to shoot out of my eyes.

"You fucking prick!!" I snarled at him. "I did not and would not even consider sleeping with your damned wife, *so stop fucking torturing me already and let me out of here!!!*"

He looked at me with hate filled eyes, let go of his dick, raised his hand and brought it down hard across my face.

"Uhhhhfffff!!!" I gasped and rolled off the tree, right into a large mud puddle on the other side of it. "Uccchhhhh!!!!"

As I lay there on my stomach in the filth with my face down in the mud Mr. Michaels came up behind me and yanked my head up by a handful of my hair.

"Arrrrhhhhh!!!" I cried as my face came up out of the mud, filth dripping off my nose, chin and mouth.

"Get on your feet you fucking waste," he ranted from behind me. "This isn't even worth it anymore."

As best a man whose feet and hands are tied I pulled myself slowly to my feet. I was covered in mud and I ached miserably all over. Mr. Michaels untied the rope around my balls, took the clothespins off my nipples and squatted down in front of me to untie my feet. I softly thanked him, but he ignored me. With his back turned to me he started walking back toward the campgrounds. I quickly trotted behind him, my hands still bound behind my back. As we walked he didn't touch me once. I guess he figured I'd had enough. I felt I'd had more than enough. We reached the campgrounds an hour and a half later. We had most likely walked for miles upon miles. Needless to say my feet were killing me. They were swollen from the humidity and I had developed a nasty shoe-bite on the heel of my left foot. Mr. Michaels untied my hands and I stood there all muddy and sexy as he looked me over.

"You look like shit Giglo," he said to me. "Fuckin' stink too."

"Yeah, I wonder why," I replied sarcastically and ran a hand through my sweat and mud soaked hair. I stood there shooing all the flies and blasted mosquitoes off me as Mr. Michaels continued looking me over, seeming to be really fascinated by my muddy and hard dick. He knew I was too winded to try to deck him. He could take me out in a microsecond if I tried anything. I didn't try anything.

"If you want to take a shower before we head back to the city," he began to say and reached and grabbed my hard dick.

"Just take me home man," I said angrily as he stroked my muddy slimy dick. "I don't want anything else from you. God knows you've given me enough shit to last a lifetime. *And let go of my damned dick.*"

With a smirk he gave my dick two hard pulls. That was all it took. He had me spewing another mess of yuppie boy jazz.

"Ohhhhrrrr GOD, you bastard!!" I grunted and he let go of my dick.

I hopped around shooting my load uncontrollably.

When I was done and as Mr. Michaels walked around to the driver's seat of the car I reached into the car's open window and pulled out my suit pants.

"Now that I'm allowed to speak do you want to know how your wife came to be in possession of my monogrammed handkerchief?" I asked him as I hopped into my suit pants.

He simply looked at me over the hood of the car.

"Last week your wife, my boss, called me into her office to discuss some new company policies regarding the customer service procedures of my job," I began. "If you recall correctly your wife had a bad cold last week. As she was speaking to me she sneezed a few times in a row. She didn't have anymore tissues in the box that was on her desk so I gave her my handkerchief to use."

Mr. Michaels seemed to look at me with regret, for all of three seconds.

"Bastard, you nearly killed me for nothing, for being a gentleman I got my damned ass kicked," I said to him angrily and grabbed my shirt out of the car and pulled it on my muddy body, leaving it hanging out of my pants. "Get me the fuck home man."

I climbed into the back seat of the car, leaned back and closed my eyes. I didn't care if I got his car all muddy and dirty, I just wanted to get home. Mr. Michaels got in the driver's seat and started the car. I dozed off for a while and when I woke up I was aching more than earlier. I realized I would need a few days to heal up.

"How did you find out my name was John Giglo?" I asked him as we drove toward my apartment building.

"After I found your handkerchief in the bedroom I went through my wife's briefcase and found her company telephone directory," he replied. "Your name was the only one with the initials JG and your name was listed under my wife's department. I looked you up in the phone book and the rest as they say is history."

"You jealous fuck," I murmured. "She should divorce you."

When we got to my apartment building I grabbed my suit jacket, my overcoat and my tie off the seat and climbed wearily out of the car. With my clothing over my arm and looking more than rumpled I sauntered over to the driver's side window.

"I just want to tell you Mr. Michaels, that if I ever see you around here or even near me I will report you and all that you did to me to the cops," I said, not looking at him. "Got it?"

In response he simply drove off, leaving me standing there looking like a muddy mess in a pair of suit pants and a shirt. I quickly trotted into my building and up to my apartment. I thanked God that my keys were still in my suit jacket pocket. Once inside I raced to the bedroom to make a phone call. She answered on the second ring.

"Hi, it's me," I said, sounding very urgent. "Listen, we have to be more careful in the future. Because of that damned handkerchief I lent you your hubby showed up here last night. And believe me, he was definitely not a happy camper."

I ran a hand through my stinking muddy hair.

"And neither was I, literally…" I said with a grin.

THE PARTY IS OVER

By Christopher Trevor

I never thought about telling this story because at first I was so mortified when it happened. But upon further recollection of the events that occurred I decided that it was actually the most erotic and titillating experience I'd ever had. And not to mention it was an experience that proved just how very potent I really can be when the chips are stacked against me. It was a Friday night and I'd been invited to a birthday party for my friend Dave at my other friend Christopher's apartment. I got stuck working late, (till about seven PM) the party was scheduled for eight PM which left me no time to neither go home and change out of my suit, nor have any dinner. At seven PM, wearing my gray pinstriped business suit I rushed out of my office, bought a present for Dave, and made it to Christopher's apartment by eight PM. In all there were eighteen people there including myself, all male. Christopher greeted me at the door with a smile on his face and a tug on my tie.

"Nice suit Carl," Christopher said. "But there was no need to get all dolled up for Dave's party. It's not a formal affair after all."

I explained how I hadn't had time to go home and change and that I hadn't had any dinner. Still holding the end of my tie in his hand Christopher told me that there was plenty of junk food around the apartment and to help myself. He also told me there was plenty of liquor and beer. I liked the sound of that. Then, Christopher let go of my tie and I walked into the apartment. (I've always known that Christopher was gay and I always had the feeling that he had a crush on me. This didn't bother me in the least, being that he is a great friend.) I ate a few chips, a couple of pretzels, and munched on one carrot stick. However, I drank can after can of beer, and had a lot of vodka and orange juices. I lost count of how many times I went to the bathroom to piss my brains out and when everyone gathered around to sit and watch Dave open his presents I watched through blurred vision. All the guys at the party cheered Dave on as he opened his presents. He received various X-rated presents that's for sure. I vaguely remember someone (I think it was Christopher) handing me another beer, and actually holding it to my lips so I could chug it down. As I slurped the beer down I heard Dave cackling that his latest gift was a vibrator. When the party was over and everyone had left it was about twelve thirty AM. I was semi conscious on the couch, (more unconscious than conscious actually) sprawled out, still wearing my complete suit, with the tie pulled down a few notches, and my top two shirt buttons undone. Through very blurred vision I saw Christopher come over to me.

"The party is over Carl," he said to me.

I smiled in my daze and a loud burp or two erupted from me.

"You're fucking plastered," Christopher said cheerfully. "But what a sight you certainly are."

The next thing I remember was Christopher helping me to my feet and then slinging me bodily over his shoulders. The room spun as he picked me up like a sack of laundry.

"Oh Gawd man, what're you doin' to me?" I slurred.

I heard Christopher saying that I would have to spend the night there as he carried me toward a bedroom. He went on to explain that I was too damned drunk to go anywhere.

"C-could've let one of your buds drive me home," I slurred softly.

"Nah, you'll be safer here," Christopher replied as he lugged me along.

The last thing I remember of that night was one of my slip-on loafers falling off my foot. Christopher carried me into his bedroom. I passed out… totally.

THE NEXT MORNING…

I woke up on Saturday morning in Christopher's bedroom. As I slowly came to (belching and farting my brains out) I realized that I was sitting in a straight back chair near Christopher's bed, wearing just my white pouch style briefs and my charcoal colored calf length dress socks. It took me a few moments to also realize that I was securely tied up to the chair. My arms were at my sides and tied off at the wrists to the back of the chair. My feet were off the floor and tied to the side rungs of the chair. I grunted miserably from the hangover pain in my head and after a while my vision cleared. As I took in the fact some more that I was tied up I sat up straight and yelled, "Christopher!!! What in all fucks is this about?!?" The bedroom door opened and Christopher walked in wearing just a pair of shorts. Smiling gleefully he sauntered over to me.

"Good morning Carl," Christopher said happily.

"What the fuck is going on man?" I asked him. "Where are my damned clothes?"

"Out in the living room," he replied. "I took the liberty of making you comfortable last night."

"By tying me up???" I blurted. "Untie me man, let me loose!! I've got to piss like a goddamned racehorse!!"

Christopher told me that he wasn't going to untie me and that I could piss into my briefs. As a matter of fact he added that he wasn't going to untie me until I had shot three loads of cum and three loads of piss into my under shorts. And when I was done he planned to keep my underpants…and then I would be free to leave…or stay around for coffee if I preferred. I could not believe what the fuck I was hearing. Piss and cum three times in my damned under shorts??? How perverted was that???

"You're fucking crazy," I said to Christopher. "Fuck, I'm not even gay! Why are you doing this man???"

"I've been wild for you for a long time Carl my boy," Christopher replied. "And yes you are gay, you're just afraid to admit it."

I gulped hard at the sound of those words because they were true.

"And there's no time like the present to get started on you," Christopher announced.

He kneeled down in front of me and began licking my already (piss) hard dick through the cotton material of my drawers.

"OHHHHH GAWD," I moaned. "Christopher, please don't do this!!"

I leaned my head back and tried to ignore what Christopher was doing but I had to admit that despite the hangover it felt fucking great! Christopher moved his hands over my legs and calves as he applied pressure to my dick with his tongue.

"OHHHHH GAWD, I'm getting close…" I moaned.

I moved my head forward to watch as Christopher lapped hungrily at my briefs covered dick. Suddenly, oh God, suddenly it was happening…I was cumming…I was fucking cumming…

"OH YEAH!!!" I screamed. "Oh yes!!! Lick my fucking dick!!! OH FUCK YEAH!!!"

Christopher watched with a smile as I jazzed like a madman into my briefs. Most of my creamy white fluid was absorbed into the cotton material but some of it seeped out. Christopher quickly licked up my seeping cum.

"Oh man, I have to admit that was fucking great!!" I said to Christopher.

"You can relieve yourself now," Christopher said to me. "I want to get started very soon on giving you your second explosion."

Embarrassment filled me but I had no choice in the matter. I pissed into my drawers, mixing my urine with my cum. Kneeling in front of me Christopher sniffed hungrily at my crotch as the yellow stream of liquid filled my underpants. I moaned contentedly and in anger as I pissed and pissed. When I was done I breathed a long sigh of relief. All at once though and even before my dick had had a chance to go soft and shriveled Christopher was licking it again…through the now soaked underpants I was wearing. To increase the mixture of pleasure and pain I was experiencing Christopher squeezed my balls and pushed my dick up and down against my skin.

"OH GAWD!!!" I yelled, feeling breathless. "OH MAN, not again so damned soon!!"

"Wait'll we get to the third blast," Christopher replied, grinning meanly up at me.

I writhed in the chair and thrashed my head back and forth as Christopher subjected me to a torture I had never known before. This was most definitely a mixture of pain and ecstasy. I tried to pull free of the ropes but they were tied too damned tight. In moments my dick was hard and cum filled again. I *would* eventually shoot a second load of jazz into my briefs. Christopher squeezed my balls harder and jacked my dick faster and faster, forcing me ever closer to shooting my load again.

"OHHHHHHH you fucker!!" I roared. "Please stop!!"

But Christopher ignored me and continued working my dick and balls really hard. Then, a few moments later the guy pressed his mouth against my balls, pushed his tongue over them, and I shot my second load of the day.

"ARRRHHHHH GOD ALMIGHTY!!!" I screamed as my cum shot out of my piss hole and into my briefs, soaking them some more.

Instead of letting go of my damned dick Christopher continued stroking it, abusing it actually. Goosebumps broke out all over my muscular body.

"OH GOD NO!!" I yelled.

All at once I was pissing again. HUMILIATING! I saw my briefs turning even more yellow as I lost control.

"Way to go Carl!" Christopher said, sounding happy but sadistic at the same time.

This time when I was done I was covered and sopped in sweat, and shaking all over I might add. I hung my head down and gasped for breath.

"P-please untie me…" I said through gasps.

Christopher stood up, rested a hand on the back of my sweat soaked neck, and gently stroked my black hair.

"I'm not going to untie you just yet Carl," he said to me. "You do have one more load to shoot for me after all."

I pulled my head up and looked at Christopher.

"I can't possibly," I whispered.

"Sure you can," Christopher said with a sneer. "I have faith in you…"

To help me out Christopher said he would get me a cold drink. That said, he left the bedroom and went out to the kitchen, leaving me alone for a few minutes. While I was by myself I struggled like crazy but in vain to get myself untied. When I tired of straining against the ropes I was sweating even more. To put it plainly I smelled rancid, a mixture of sweat, cum and piss all emanating from me. Christopher returned carrying two cold cans of beer. He held them up in front of me.

"To quench your thirst Carl," he said to me. "Your hot thirst that is…"

"BEER???" I yelled. "At this time of day??? GEEZ man, my head is already spinning like a top!! What in all fucks are you trying to do to me???"

Without a word Christopher put one of the cans of beer down on the floor, opened the other one, yanked my head back by a handful of my hair, and forced me to drink, or should I say guzzle. I was too weak to resist so I simply did as Christopher wished. The first can of beer was gone in three gulps and I started feeling drunk all over again. Christopher cupped my chin in his hand, smiled mockingly at me, and I belched really loud and disgusting. My so called buddy laughed meanly, tossed the empty beer can to the floor and grabbed one of my nipples real hard.

"OWWWWWW!!!" I bellowed in a sort of drunken stupor.

As Christopher squeezed and twisted my nipple real hard and as I yelled loudly in pain, my mouth wide open, Christopher quickly placed a tiny blue pill atop my tongue.

"H-hey…" I managed to say and as I went to spit out whatever the pill was Christopher let go of my nipple, placed one hand on top of my head and the other hand back under my chin.

The guy pressed down hard on the top of my head, his fingers twined in my hair, and pushed upwards from under my chin. I involuntarily clamped my mouth shut, no chance now of spitting out the tiny blue pill.

"MMMMMMRRRRRRMMMMMMM…" I groaned as Christopher held tight to my head and chin, not allowing me to open my mouth.

I felt the tiny pill dissolve in my mouth…

"WHAT THE FUCK MAN???" I sputtered angrily when Christopher let go of my head and chin, him sure that the pill was gone and swallowed by yours truly here.

"Nothing to worry about Carl," Christopher mused, ruffling my sweat sopped hair.

"Look buddy, I may drink and party and all that good stuff, but I don't do drugs," I snarled.

"Relax, it's not going to hurt you, actually, it'll enhance you," Christopher replied and picked up the second can of beer he had brought into the bedroom with him.

The guy was right, because as I watched him open the can of beer I suddenly felt an immense tingling in my cock as it rested in my cum and pissed soaked briefs.

"OOOOOOO, oh holy shit man, what, what in all fucks did you make me swallow here Christopher?" I asked, feeling all sleazy in my under shorts.

"Good old fashioned Viagra buddy," Christopher said with a grin and held up the second can of beer.

"VIAGRA???" I gurgled and then Christopher was holding the second can of beer to my mouth.

He forced me to guzzle the second can down also…

When I was done with both beers and the Viagra pill I was drunk as a skunk, horny as a toad and my head was spinning like crazy. I saw Christopher through blurred vision, him again laughing at me. He leaned down and kissed me gently on the lips. I was surprised to find myself responding to the guy's kisses by pushing my numb tongue into his mouth. My cock was beefy and hard in my underpants. We stopped after about five kisses and then Christopher started on my dick again, my rock hard dick to put it plainly, licking it through the cotton material of my soaked drawers. Horny as I was my head lolled around on my shoulders and even in my drunken stupor I realized that the Viagra tablet had done its job…because I was fucking harder than hard even after having shot two man sized loads already.

"WH-why don't you take it out and suck it?" I slurred.

"Maybe another time Carl," Christopher responded. "For now I want those briefs of yours smelling good."

"There won't be a next time," I said slowly.

"Oh yes there will," Christopher said with a grin. "After this you won't be able to resist me…ever."

I watched in my drunken and horned up stupor as my dick became harder and harder under my briefs as Christopher licked it like a madman. Then, he grabbed my nuts and twisted them painfully, not stopping his tongue for a second. I screamed in pain and ecstasy at the same time. Christopher rocked my dick up and down by my nuts and a few moments later I came for the third time in less than an hour…of course the Viagra that Christopher had forced down my throat did help me along somewhat. I thrashed wildly in the chair as my juices smeared my briefs some more.

"OH GAWD, I'm fucking cumming again!" I screamed.

This time when I was done I hung my head down and gasped like crazy for breath. Christopher kissed my balls and my thighs. I was sweating like crazy…

"Un-untie me…" I pleaded.

I smelled like a goddamned shithouse. Christopher wrapped his hand once again around my dick and said one word to me… "Piss." I grimaced and forced every drop of the yellow urine out of myself and into my briefs, still panting for breath. When I was totally drained Christopher untied my feet and slowly pulled my sopped underpants off me. My dick was half hard, half soft. Christopher gave it a kiss. Next, he untied my hands and sat down on the bed, facing me as I massaged my wrists. Christopher held my briefs protectively in his hands.

"You can take a shower before you leave," Christopher said to me.

I stood up slowly and walked to the bathroom…

Later on that morning Christopher and I ate breakfast together in a local restaurant. My suit pants felt strange on me without my underpants on but Christopher truly insisted on keeping them and he didn't have any of his that would fit me…or so he said. Somehow I think it turned the sleazy guy on knowing I was sitting there in a suit with no goddamned underpants on.

After a lot of coffee I finally sobered up. Christopher invited me back to his place for more fun and I admit that I took him up on his invitation…

A year later Christopher and I are still together. Actually, we've been lovers ever since…

SPANKING BILL

By Christopher Trevor

A roll of the dice will determine your spanking fate," Chris said to me as I stood next to him with my hands cuffed in front of myself.

I was wearing just a pair of silk teal colored boxer briefs with three buttons in the front instead of a fly opening, (at the moment the buttons were unbuttoned, exposing my big hard Irish dick) a pair of black knee length (OTC) nylon ribbed dress socks, and black spit shined lace-up wingtip shoes. I felt utterly ridiculous and sexy at the same time all dressed up in such a humiliating fashion. Chris handed me two dice and I gulped hard in fear as he placed a hand on my shoulder.

"Remember the rules," Chris reminded me. "If you roll double numbers you'll receive twice that number's swats with my leather paddle. So in other words if you roll two fives you'll receive twenty swats instead of ten.

Chris squeezed one of my sexy butt cheeks and I turned my head, looking at him imploringly, playing my part very well.

"Roll the dice…" Chris said softly directly into my ear.

As I shook the dice in my cuffed hands I remembered the moment I had arrived at Chris' apartment for one of our erotic encounters. We've been doing this sort of thing for a while now and have come to call our times together our "Erotic Encounters." Sometimes I spend a good amount of time tied to a chair as Chris parades around the house practically naked, showing off his excellent body. My dick throbs like crazy as I sit there bound to the chair until Chris decides to give me release. He loves making me wait. Other times I'm blindfolded and stretched out on the bed as Chris licks my sexy feet, sometimes with my black nylon socks on, sometimes with them off, sometimes after licking my feet with my socks on he'll roll the socks off me and then lick my bare sweaty tootsies. The deal with that is that Chris gets to keep my smelly socks after he's done servicing them. I have no problem with that, seeing as, like most guys, I have mounds of black socks. This time I am a little nervous because Chris has decided that he wants to give me a spanking, er, spankings. He wants to give me spankings. In return he said he'll lick my feet and milk my cock. I had not shot a load in a few days (per Chris' orders) so my cock was really more than hard when I arrived at Chris' apartment that day. I was wearing a blue business suit (also per Chris' instructions) and Chris took his time slowly stripping me out of it… down to my silk underpants and shoes and socks. He then cuffed my hands in front of me and felt me up all over, running and trailing his hands up and down my muscular arms, squeezing my biceps, squeezing my bubble butt, and slapping my tree trunk-like thighs a few times. He unbuttoned my three button boxer briefs and out popped my big hard dick. It was oozing pre-cum and throbbing with a life of its own. Chris licked the tiny droplets of pre-cum from my piss hole and then walked me over to the coffee table where the dice were. On the couch I saw the round leather paddle that I would be swatted with, and swatted with, and swatted with. I continued shaking up the dice, taking my time about it.

"Take all the time you want…" Chris said as he stroked my silky black hair. "We have all day after all."

He was right about that. I had arrived at his apartment at nine AM on the dot after having ridden the train with all the other business suited men. If only they knew that I was suited up for a day of bondage, spanking, and having my cock milked numerous times. Chris loves milking me numerous times. He says that watching me shoot a giant load of creamy goo always charges his batteries. When he gets to the third time he keeps me tightly tied up so

I can't stop him from milking me like crazy. At this point he also keeps me blindfolded so I can concentrate on what he's doing to me.

"Roll the dice…" Chris said sternly.

I kneeled over the coffee table and dropped the dice out of my cuffed hands. Chris and I both looked at the five and the two.

"Seven," Chris said. "A lucky start."

I stood up, faced Chris, and kissed him on the lips. Then, he took me by one arm, walked me over to the couch and laid me over his knees, my ass right over his lap. My dick was dangling between his parted legs, touching only the air. Chris didn't want my dick rubbing against anything. He didn't want me to have any chance whatsoever of jerking myself off. My pleasures would come later. He picked up the leather paddle.

"The first spanking will be with your boxer briefs up, the next spanking will be with the boxer briefs pulled down," Chris said and brought the paddle down hard on my butt cheeks.

"Owwwwww!!!" I yelled in pain. "One Sir!!"

I had been instructed to count off each swat I received and to call Chris "Sir" after each number. He swatted my butt again.

"Owwwwww!!! Two Sir!!" I railed in pain.

He swatted my butt again, harder on the third swat.

"UHHHHH…three Sir!!" I said through clenched teeth.

SWAT!!!!!!

"Four, Sir!!" I cried.

When Chris reached the seventh swat he told me to stand back up. He stood up next to me and handed me the dice again. I kissed his lips twice and he squeezed my already stinging butt.

"Come on Billy boy, roll a really high number," Chris said teasingly.

Again I kneeled over the coffee table, shook up the dice, and dropped them on the table. My eyes opened wide in fear and Chris' eyes opened wide in delight as we looked at the double sixes I had rolled.

"No, no!!" I said loudly as I stood up and faced Chris.

"Oh yeah you mean…" Chris said, smiling fiendishly.

He took me again by my arm and walked me over to the couch.

"Ahhhh fuck man," I whimpered dejectedly, my ass cheeks twitching already with the anticipation of what was coming.

Moments later I was over Chris' knees again, this time with my boxer briefs pulled down in the back, exposing my creamy white ass cheeks. By the way, Chris loves my ass. It's a bubble butt, smooth as a bowl of whipped cream. One time in the past when we had gotten together Chris spent a good deal of time licking, kissing, drooling and bighting on my ass. This time the fucker was spending a good deal of time spanking my hot ass, fucking torturing me in a way. Chris gave my sexy buns a few squeezes, a few kisses, and a lot of licks (for the moment with his tongue) before he began spanking me. Then, he picked up his leather paddle and began swatting me.

"OWWWWWW!!!" I screamed. "One Sir!!!"

He swatted my butt again.

"OWWWWW!!!" I cried out. "Two Sir!!!"

Again he swatted my butt, harder this time.

"TH-Three Sir!!!" I yelled in pain.

When he got to the twelfth swat my ass cheeks were already red and I was fighting back tears. Chris stopped for half a minute to allow me to catch my breath.

"Doing well so far Billy boy," Chris teased me.

"TH-thank you Sir!!" I replied.

He rubbed the palm of his hand over my red butt cheeks.

"Feeling hot back here Billy boy," he teased me some more.

"Yes Sir!!" I said.

Chris lifted one of my legs back by the ankle and took a long sniff of my black sock. Then, he lowered my leg back down and brought the paddle down on my ass for the thirteenth swat. I screamed in pain and said, "Thirteen Sir!!"

Smiling, Chris' dick was hard in his jeans as he swatted my butt mercilessly till he reached the twenty fourth swats. When he was done my ass was beyond red. It was crimson. He put the paddle down and rubbed a good amount of some aloe cream over my ass cheeks.

"TH-thank you Sir, that feels good," I whimpered as tears slid down my cheeks.

Chris stuck a greasy finger in my asshole a few times and I thanked him for that also, telling him how good it felt. Then, he pulled my boxer briefs back up over my ass cheeks.

"On your feet," Chris ordered.

I stood up. My dick was still hard as a fucking rock and throbbing. Despite the pain from the spankings I had received so far it had not gone down once.

"Are you okay so far?" Chris asked me, stepping behind me.

He held me by my arms, squeezing my muscles.

"Y-yeah, I'm alright," I replied. "But my ass feels like it's on fire."

"And we've only gotten started," Chris said and squeezed my arms tighter. "Okay Bill, for the next spanking round I'm going to gag you."

"Why?" I asked him. "You never gag me."

"Two reasons," Chris replied. "First, for the next round I'm going to spank you harder than before and I don't want the neighbors hearing you scream and cry. So you better hope you roll a low number on the dice. Second, I have a more than ripe pair of my sweat socks from yesterday waiting for you in the hamper."

"Shit, shit, shit…" I said as Chris went to the hamper in the bathroom.

In moments I had a rolled up white cotton sweat sock crammed in my mouth and another one tied over it, jamming it firmly in place. I stood next to Chris with an angry looking expression on my face.

"I bet those socks taste good huh?" Chris asked me mockingly. "I wore them all day yesterday and then while I was working out at the gym. Man, I was fucking sweating like crazy…"

I rolled my eyes and looked away from him. The sweat socks tasted rancid, to put it bluntly. Yet I was totally turned on by the taste of them and totally turned on by the torture that Chris was dishing out on me.

"After this round of spanking I'll service your feet Billy boy, socks on first," Chris said to me. "Then I'll spank you again and service your feet again, socks off."

I smiled through the gag and Chris handed me the dice.

"Decide your spanking fate…" he said to me.

I shook up the dice in my still cuffed hands and squatted down. I dropped the dice on the coffee table. I had rolled a three and a one.

"Lucky guy you are," Chris said to me as I stood up.

He grabbed me by my arms, whirled me around, and kissed me on my sock gagged mouth.

"Fucking going to give you four hard swats Billy Boy," Chris said threateningly.

My dick throbbed hard and feverishly, begging to shoot its pent-up load at this point. Then, Chris had me over his knees and the paddle was in his hand. I braced myself. He brought the paddle down on my butt, hard, really fucking hard.

"RRRMMMFFFF!!!" was all I could say in pain.

"What was that?" Chris asked me teasingly. "I couldn't quite hear you Billy boy."

He swatted my butt again, harder than the first time.

"MMMMFFFF!!!" I sputtered into the gag.

"Still couldn't hear you…" Chris said and pulled my boxer briefs down in the back.

He swatted my ass a third time and I sputtered again into the sock gag in total pain. I cried profusely, tears streaming down my cheeks like crazy. I tasted the sweat from Chris' sweat sock in my mouth and it was driving me ape shit. Chris gave my ass the fourth and hardest swat yet.

"RRRRRRMMMMMFFFF!!!!" I cried out and looked back at him beseechingly.

"Time for a break…" he said, rubbing a hand over my much wounded butt.

I nodded in agreement as Chris put the paddle down. A short while later I was sitting on the couch with my feet propped up on the coffee table on a big white pillow. The socks were out of my mouth and now my hands were cuffed behind me. Chris didn't want me going near my dick until he said that it was okay to do so. Still, my dick was out of my briefs and hard, hard, hard. I watched as Chris slowly untied my shoelaces and slipped my wingtips just as slowly off my feet. He sniffed the inside of each shoe before laying it on the floor.

"Beg me to lick your damned feet..." Chris said as he ran a hand over my right socked foot.

"Please Sir, lick my feet," I pleaded. "It feels so good when you do it."

Chris smiled and sniffed one of my feet.

"They stink," he said. "What will you offer me in return for licking those stinking feet of yours?"

"I'll be glad to let you paddle my sore ass again Sir!" I replied.

Chris smiled and leaned forward. He began slowly licking my right socked foot, savoring the taste of it.

"MMMM..." Chris crooned as his tongue glided up the side of my right foot.

"Ohhh...feels so good," I whispered.

He sucked on my smelly dress socks as he massaged my feet with his fingertips. I closed my eyes and leaned my head back. I drifted in ecstasy. Chris sucked my toes through the thin nylon material of my socks and gulped down his saliva. I could see the tell-tale bulge in his jeans growing larger.

"Why don't you jack yourself off Sir?" I asked Chris.

Without a word Chris stood up, pulled his big meat from his jeans and began slowly stroking his huge hard cock.

"Oh yeah, going to fucking cream all over your damned socks," Chris said breathlessly. "Going to have those socks of yours smelling real good Billy boy..."

In a few minutes Chris shot his load, letting it stream over my feet. It was very erotic looking the way his hot white load dripped all over my black socks.

"Oh yeah, yeah!!!" Chris moaned in a man's ecstasy as he milked every drop of cum from his big hard cock.

Then, I watched as Chris knelt back down at my feet and began licking his hot cum off my socks, slowly, savoring the taste of his juices and my feet sweat. As I sat there watching my erotic master lick my smelly feet I wondered just which one of us really was the master. Who was more in control of this scene? Was it Chris who was delighting in tormenting me, spanking me, and keeping my hands cuffed? Or was it me? Even though I'd been stripped to my underpants and socks was I the one controlling this? Then I thought what did it matter as long we were both feeling totally great? Chris licked and licked his cum off the fronts of my feet and worked his tongue slowly over the bottoms of them. I wiggled my toes under my socks as Chris got close to finishing with my feet. When he was done he slipped my wingtips back onto my feet and tied the laces.

"Okay Billy boy, back up on your feet," Chris ordered. "Its time again to roll the dice and see how many swats you're going to get this time…"

"Shit…" I whispered as I pulled myself to my feet.

Chris un-cuffed one of my hands and pulled my hands back in front of me where he cuffed them again.

"Roll the dice," Chris said, handing me the dice.

I looked at him, rolled the dice in my hands, and knelt over the coffee table. I dropped the dice on the table. When Chris saw the double fives I had rolled he let out a whoop of joy and excitement.

"*Shit, shit, shit…* " I whimpered, still on my knees and looking hatefully at the two dice.

Chris pulled me to my feet and then hoisted me a few inches off the floor by my butt cheeks.

"Fucking twenty swats you're in for Billy boy!!" Chris hooted happily.

He carried me around the room like a sack of laundry and then settled down on the couch with me splayed across his knees, my ass on his lap again. He pulled my boxer briefs down in the back and rubbed my buns with the palm of his hand.

"Man, your fucking ass is really going to shine now Billy boy," Chris said jokingly.

"Please, please Chris, take it easy during this round," I said, looking back at him beseechingly.

"Face forward Billy boy!!" Chris said as he picked up the leather paddle.

"Yes Sir!!" I replied and did as I was told.

Chris brought the paddle down on my butt, hard, but not as hard as earlier.

"OWWWWW!!!" I cried loudly anyway. "One Sir!!"

My already crimson red ass was going to be even more crimson by the time this was over I thought. Chris swatted me a second time.

"YOWWWW!!! Two Sir!!!" I yelped.

At the tenth swat Chris stopped for a half a minute to allow me again to catch my breath. My teeth were clenched and I was crying, tears streaming down my cheeks.

"Please Sir; take it easy on the next ten swats…" I pleaded. *"Please…"*

"I love it when you beg…" Chris commented fiendishly.

He picked up the paddle and swatted my ass for the eleventh time.

"Eleven Sir!!!" I cried through my clenched teeth.

Another swat, not so hard but stinging all the same.

"Twelve Sir!!!" I roared.

When Chris was done I laid still across his lap as he again rubbed the soothing aloe lotion over my ass cheeks. They felt like they were more than red and wounded. The guy had really worked me over this time out. Then, Chris pulled my boxer briefs back up in the rear and told me to stand up. I stood and he stood in front of me. I shook and sobbed as he kissed me on the lips, hugged me close, and massaged the back of my neck.

"Th-thank you Sir…thank you…" I whispered.

Moments passed and then I was again sitting on the couch with my feet propped up on the pillow. This time Chris had left my hands cuffed in front of me. I watched for the second time as he slowly unlaced my wingtips and slipped them off my feet. Then, he put them down on the floor and squeezed my socked feet, giving them a kiss each.

"Mmmm…love your feet…" Chris crooned, sniffing my smelly socks.

"You said that you would service my feet socks off this time," I reminded my master.

"You really want another spanking don't you?" Chris asked me, sounding threatening.

"No Sir, no, I don't…" I said apologetically.

"I'll get these stinking socks off your feet when I'm good and fucking ready," Chris said. "Is that clear?"

"Yes Sir!!" I replied.

Then, Chris rolled my socks off my feet and the smell of foot sweat assaulted both our noses. Chris gave one of my big toes a suck.

"Jack off while I lick your damned smelly feet," Chris ordered. "And if you cum fast enough I may not spank you again…"

I grabbed my hard cock and Chris began licking my sweaty feet, trailing and running his tongue all over them and gulping down his saliva. I wanted to jack off slowly, to savor it, but I knew that if I did that Chris would spank me again. And with my luck I would either roll a high number on the dice or possibly roll double sixes. And my ass cheeks were red enough thank you very much. I stroked my cock faster. And then, as I watched Chris service my feet I shot a giant load of cum all over my smooth hairless chest.

"OHHHHHHH yeah, yeah," I cried out in a man's passion. "Oh fucking yes!!!"

Chris ran the tip of his tongue over the bottom of my right foot as I shot and shot my load.

"OHHHH yeah," I crooned softly as the last droplets of cum erupted from my cock.

When I was done I leaned back on the couch, relaxed and feeling great. Chris looked up at me, his hands wrapped around one of my feet.

"Looks like you need a shower Billy boy," Chris commented.

We smiled at each other. I stood up, Chris un-cuffed my hands, I pulled my boxer briefs off, and together we walked to the bathroom to shower together.

THE RETURN OF THE TICKLE MEISTER

By Adam Nicks and added onto by Christopher Trevor

Setting: New York City, Manhattan Detention Center, where Adam H. (AKA the Tickle Meister) is being detained and questioned by a new guard by the name of Rick Marshall...

"So tell me Adam, what brings you to New York City?" the dashingly handsome Rick Marshall asked the Tickle Meister.

"Business, *business* brings me to New York City," the Meister replied, eyeing the handsome guard inquisitively.

"Really?" Rick asked. "Because my report here says that you intend to open a shop of some kind. Is that correct?"

"Yes, that is correct," the Meister said. "You might say I intend to open a sweet shop."

Rick smiled, a beguilingly handsome smile the Meister realized and said, "Shops like that are a dime a dozen here."

The Meister gripped his classy looking walking stick and said, "Well, not the kind of sweets I sell." Rick realized that the Meister was leering at him, gulped out loud and asked, "And what kind of sweets might that be Adam?"

Adam smiled a bit coyly and said, "Perhaps maybe, *just maybe,* you might find out one day what kind of sweets I intend to sell in my shop."

Rick nearly groaned at the Meister's reply, realizing that he was not going to get any definitive answers from this man. He knew his legal rights. Even though the Meister had been arrested on a charge of supposedly breaking and entering he knew that he did not *have to* answer any questions put to him by this cop or anyone else for that matter. The guard cleared his throat and said, "Well, do you know why you were brought here today?"

"Yes, indeed I do know, I was brought here on some foolish, made up charge I am sure," the Meister responded, sounding very bored now. "To be more precise Adam, you were brought here for breaking and entering an empty warehouse." Rick said sternly.

"As I said a made up charge," the Meister repeated. "According to one of your former employees here named Clyde Wheeler, that buffoon! He can't even tie his own shoelaces let alone be an eyewitness, please Rick. That is your name isn't it?"

"Yes, my name is Rick, but you can call me Officer Marshall," Rick said.

"Then seeing as we are going by titles here I suppose you can call me "Tickle Meister", Adam said and Rick's heart dropped to his booted feet.

Rick wiggled his toes nervously in his boots and asked, "Did you just say "Tickle Meister?"

"Yes, that's right," Adam replied, grinning wickedly now at Rick's stunned reaction.

Rick, the handsomer than handsome security guard had heard talk of the man who called himself "The Tickle Meister", but he always dismissed it as petty gossip and hearsay, plus, being as ticklish as he was himself just the thought of being captured and tickle tortured was enough to make his skin crawl. The guard again wiggled his toes nervously in his boots.

"So, so you're the one who goes around managing to somehow steal men's shoes and socks and even go so far as to capture and tickle torture them?!?" Rick asked incredulously, feeling his own booted feet become even warmer. "What in all hell is that about???"

"Really, must you ask these questions?" Adam asked the guard, sounding totally annoyed now. "You said I was brought here on a charge of breaking and entering. Now you're talking about me capturing and tickle torturing men and stealing their shoes and socks. Which is it you want me here for? You're beginning to bore me."

"Oh, is that so?" Rick asked, starting to get angry now.

"Yes indeed, I suppose it must be a trend among cops, always repeating yourselves," Adam laughed and wagged a finger at Rick.

"Hey!!" the guard said as he shot from his chair. "Now that's below the belt Mister Meister, heh, I like that, Mister Meister."

"Hmm, glad to know I'm on target," the Meister said teasingly, looking at the wondrous form that was Rick's package between his muscular legs encased in his dark uniform trousers.

"Meaning what?" Rick asked, as if he didn't know.

The Meister chuckled and said, "I always go for the jewels."

"OKAY, now you're starting to piss me off!" Rick said as he glared at the Meister.

At that moment two more guards entered the interrogation room. The Meister read their nametags. One read "T. Backman" and the other "J. Carlson."

"What's going on in here" Backman asked, seeing that Rick was all flustered, angry, and not to mention somehow hot and bothered, which the Meister rather enjoyed.

He very much enjoyed seeing the handsome Rick's nerves frayed…

Once again Rick took a deep breath and made the introductions. Everyone sat down and the interrogation of the Meister continued…

The Meister thought to himself how very interesting it was to have three handsome guards with big blue eyes and big black booted feet questioning him. And how delectable he thought as well when he glanced at J. Carlson and noticed him watching him intently. The Meister grinned wickedly, uttered a low groan and became a tad dizzy.

"So Adam," T. Backman asked now. "You call yourself "The Tickle Meister." Why?"

"Why do you think Officer Backman?" the Meister replied sarcastically.

"Just answer the question Adam," Officer Backman seethed.

"I just did…*my dear Timmy*," Adam sneered, grinning at the same time.

T. Backman narrowed his eyes, wondered how this guy knew his first name and said, "Alright Adam, we can do this easy or we can do this rough."

"Oh really Timmy, must this bogus interrogation go on any longer?" the Meister asked.

"Oh trust me, it will go on and on all night if need be Adam," Timmy said.

Just then, a knock on the door was heard and another officer entered the interrogation room.

"I got news, someone posted his bail," the guard at the door announced, holding up a document that had been signed by a court judge.

"Who posted his damned bail?" Timmy asked in disbelief.

The guard said, "Someone named Christopher Trevor," and then left. The Meister had the pleasure of seeing the three guards, Rick, T. Backman and J. Carlson look shell shocked and completely stupid…

"Well gentlemen, I bid you a good day," the Meister said with obvious pleasure as he rose to leave, gripping his walking stick.

As he reached the door his upper arm was caught in an iron-like grip. Looking quickly to see who had seized him, the Meister saw that it was the handsome Officer Backman.

"Well really Officer, what can you possibly be up to?" the Meister asked, sounding very irritated now.

"You're not going anywhere," Timmy said with an evil blue eyed glare.

"Oh, is that so?" the Meister asked. "Well, my bail was posted so there really is no need to detain me any longer."

"He's right Timmy, let him go," J. Carlson said.

"The boy makes sense," Adam said to Timmy. "Now, will you kindly let go of my arm?"

Timmy gave the Meister a hard once over with his piercing blue eyes and whispered, "You think I don't remember you eh Adam?" and then out loud said, "Alright, but you haven't seen the last of me. We will meet again." As Timmy spoke he had a cold glaring look on his face.

"Indeed we will," the Meister said with a smirk on his face. "And to see that that meeting does indeed happen I would like to invite you to the grand opening of my candy shop in a week."

He handed the three officers his business card.

"I really do hope you can all make it," he went on, looking especially at Timmy. "I promise you will have a ticklish good time. Until then TTFN."

That said the Meister raised his walking stick and closed the door behind him…

As Timmy sank back into his chair his cop buddies looked at him questioningly…

Later that night the Meister returned to his luxury apartment on Fifth Avenue. As he made his way to his bedroom he sensed that someone was there. He threw the door open, expecting to deal with an intruder but stopped short when he saw a shirt on the floor, followed by a man's black dress shoe and then a black sock, then the other shoe with the other sock stuffed inside it. When the Meister rounded the corner of his bedroom he saw sprawled out on his bed, bare chested and barefooted, Officer J. Carlson, looking rather devilish.

"So what kept you?" the cop asked with a sinister looking grin. "Perhaps the real question of the hour Sir is, what the hell are you doing here?" the Meister asked.

"You mean you're not happy to see me?" Carlson asked and gave his bulge a squeeze, his erection paramount.

"If I want happy I'll go to Disney Land," the Meister replied.

"Now Adam, that's not nice," J. Carlson replied. "Anyway, I could be a lot more fun than Disney land. And I don't charge admission."

Carlson wiggled his eyebrows with a naughty looking smirk.

"Well dear boy, as fun as that sounds I would hate to wear you out before eight PM on a Friday night…" the Meister said.

"HEY!!! I can last!!" the naked cop blurted angrily.

The Meister laughed and said, "You couldn't last five minutes with what I would put you through cop!"

Officer Carlson narrowed his blue eyes and said, "Is that so? You want to try me?"

"Now, Now, Jonathan, temper, temper," the Meister said teasingly, calling the cop by his first name just to unnerve him, as he had done earlier with the handsome Officer T. Backman.

Before the Meister could stop him though, Jonathan grabbed him and yanked him down on the bed, pinning him with his own well-toned muscular body…

"Now you listen to me Meister," Jonathan said through clenched teeth. "The only reason I came here tonight is to see you and to let you know that I'm gaga over you. "When I saw you sitting in that interrogation room today I almost drooled and gave myself away."

"Oh? Would you like a bib?" the Meister asked the cop mockingly.

Jonathan got up and yanked the Meister along with him.

"Alright Adam, that's it, I've been nice, I've been patient, but you're really pushing my goddamned buttons here," the cop reeled.

"Ah, then be sure to let me know when I get the jackpot," Adam, AKA the Meister replied with a chuckle.

"Damn you man!!" Jonathan roared and pulled Adam to him and kissed him hard on the mouth.

When the cop lifted his head and looked at Adam he groaned and said, "Man, I needed that…"

"Did you?" Adam asked, licking his lips.

"Hell yeah," the cop said. "As I was saying before you opened you smart mouth I want to be your next victim."

"Careful Jonathan, just be very careful, because what you wish for you just might get," Adam said in warning.

Then, he started to back the cop against the bed. He pushed him down. Jonathan's blue eyes opened wide and he said, "Hey, what's going on?" and then watched in horror what Adam was doing. Shit, he was cuffing him to the bedposts.

"Hey, where did those come from?" John asked. "Where did you get them?"

"Never you mind," Adam said. "Now, you said you wanted to be my next victim eh? Well then, now I'm going to show you why I'm called "The Tickle Meister." "I gave you a fair chance to escape…yet you stayed. Not wise my boy, not wise at all… Ever since I saw you in those black boots you wear with your cop uniform I wondered what those feet of yours looked and smelled like…"

With an evil looking grin on his face The Meister grabbed Jonathan's left foot and sniffed underneath his toes. Jonathan groaned and thought how very proud his buddy Christopher Trevor would be of him right about now…

"HEY!!!" the cop suddenly blurted, knowing he had to play his part in this ticklish scenario. "Adam, you cut that out now!! Okay, okay man, I'll leave if you release me, please!"

The cop was begging.

"As I said, you had your chance to leave before but you chose not to," The Meister said, tickling Jonathan's toes, then stopped and decided to have a lick, which the cop groaned at aloud and that pleased The Meister very much.

Then, when Adam looked up he saw Jonathan watching him, his blue eyes still glazed over, which was how Adam intended to keep him…weak and dazed from ecstasy.

Meanwhile, Timmy Backman decided to enter the home of the Meister as well. No one seemed to recall the last time that he and the Meister had met. But the guard remembered it well, and he planned to have the Meister pay for having subjected his thin socked feet to relentless tickle tortures. He had come prepared to pick the lock on the Meister's door but luck seemed to be on the handsome guard's side, as he found the door open and as soon as he closed the door behind him he realized he was not alone. Noises were coming from down the hall of the apartment. Being a cop and having been an army reservist and waiting for another showdown with the Meister Timmy ventured down the hallway. But he could not do so unarmed so he picked up the bluntest object he could lay his hands on, an iron skillet and then made his way slowly to the master bedroom where the noises were coming from. Being an auxiliary cop Timmy was not permitted to carry a firearm. The door to the Meister's bedroom was cracked and Timmy waited and listened some more. The sounds he heard were of someone moaning in pain. He slipped inside and noticed a shirt and tie and black shoes and socks on the floor and then went in a little further. Around the corner Timmy stopped dead in his tracks…he saw Officer Jonathan Carlson being foot worshiped by the Meister himself…

Timmy's blood boiled hot, not sure why, but he somehow felt jealous. He thundered into the room the rest of the way, raised the skillet, prepared to send it crashing down on the Meister's head, but waited, as he watched the Meister continue to toy with Jonathan. The Meister then had Jonathan sit up and as the cop did he saw Timmy and his eyes opened wide. Adam noticed the look on Jonathan's face and turned and ducked quickly out of the way as Timmy sent the skillet crashing down not on his head, but on unsuspecting Officer Carlson's, knocking the cop out cold and sending him off to dreamland…

"Oh double damn!!" Adam shouted, got up and tried to run, but Timmy's muscular arm shot out and caught him and reeled him in like a fish. "Hey, let me go!! How dare you???"

Timmy let the Meister drop like a sack of meal to the floor…

The Meister turned around, faced the cop and glared at him.

"How dare you???" he shouted a second time, taking in the sight of the unconscious Officer Carlson.

"You already said that," Timmy said with a leer. "FUCK, that skillet was meant for you Meister!"

The Meister laughed meanly and said, "Um, hate to break this to you but you missed flatfoot!!" Now very angry, Timmy advanced on Adam and tried to nail him but it was not working… The man who called himself the Meister was just too quick on his feet and nimble it seemed…

Meanwhile, Adam's buddy, the author Christopher Trevor had decided to pay Adam a visit and when he got to his door, like Timmy before him, he heard commotion coming from the back of the apartment. He went in slowly to check it out and saw a man in a cop uniform trying to strangle Adam. Seeing his buddy in trouble Christopher figured it was a tickle scene gone wrong and that the man really was not a cop, but just role-playing, the author tried to pull him off but had no luck. Whoever he was he was hell bent on strangling the life out of Adam. So Christopher proceeded to grab the bogus cop around the neck and finally managed to pry him off and away from Adam…

With his back still to his buddy Timmy tried to shake Christopher off but was not successful. If anything, Christopher's hold became tighter and Timmy was not even able to yell out that it was him, Timmy Backman, Christopher's good buddy. Timmy finally had had enough and yanked Christopher roughly off him, sending him flying onto the bed. Then, Timmy went to have another go at Adam as he saw the guy trying to get to his feet and escape. As Adam did get to his feet Timmy yelled out, "Oh no you don't Meister!" and yanked Adam's ankles out from under him and sent the guy sprawling to the floor. This though was in Adam's favor because he landed right near his night table, and beside that night table was his ever-trusty walking stick. As Timmy closed in on him Adam grabbed the walking stick, turned around and raised it, pointing it directly at Timmy's handsome face.

"Don't try it Backman," Adam said, his hand shaking as he pointed the walking stick at Timmy.

"And what are you going to do with that Adam?" Timmy laughed. "Poke me?"

"Don't give me any naughty ideas Sir," the Meister said threateningly.

Timmy, hell bent on his revenge on the Meister advanced some more, made to grab him, but Adam raised his walking stick higher and pressed the button at the top of it. A sickly scented gas shot out of the walking stick's tip which caught the unsuspecting Timmy full on in the face. His eyes began to close as he involuntarily inhaled and he slowly dropped to the floor, now on his way to dreamland…

"Ah, now that he's out of the way how about a drink my friend?" Adam asked Christopher.

Looking at Adam in disbelief Christopher said, "You shouldn't have done that man…"

"And why is that?" Adam asked in reply.

"Well, I do have a confession to make," Christopher said. "I knew you planned to capture him again and I came here to rescue him from you…"

"Oh and how did you plan on doing that?" Adam asked.

"Well, overpower you and then take Timmy with me," Christopher said with a grin.

"Hmmm…interesting," Adam said. "Well, here's your drink Mr. Author."

Christopher took the glass and asked, "What is this Adam?"

"Just red wine, I know how much you enjoy a glass of it every once in a while," Adam said with a warm smile.

Christopher watched Adam move Timmy over to the bed and bind his wrists up to the frame.

"Adam, what are you doing?" Christopher asked.

"Preparing for phase two of my plan," Adam replied with a naughty looking smirk on his face.

Just then, a groan came from Officer Carlson. Adam quickly gave him a dose of the knockout gas from his walking stick, sending the poor cop back to dreamland. Jonathan groaned miserably as he drifted back to sleep. Adam chuckled. Now Timmy was starting to come to as well.

"Well, well, and just in time," Adam said and looked over at Christopher as he sipped his wine, the author somehow fascinated by the goings-on in the bedroom as the Meister took control of the entire situation…and the men in the room. "Well Christopher, you look a little wobbly as well. You might want to sit down. How is that wine by the way?"

At that question the author narrowed his brown eyes.

"Adam, what the hell did you do?" Christopher asked.

"Do?" Adam asked.

"Answer my damned question Adam!!" Christopher demanded, angry now.

"I simply gave you a glass of red wine," Adam replied.

"A glass of red wine and what else???" Christopher barked.

"Oh, I did forget to mention that the wine was laced with a special serum," Adam laughed.

Christopher's jaw dropped.

"What the hell kind of serum?" Christopher asked incredulously.

"The kind that renders the recipient of it under my complete and total control," Adam replied, once again grinning evilly.

"You bastard!!" Christopher shouted. "You drugged me? ME??? How dare you man???"

"Now, now Mr. Author, temper, temper, or should I say Mr. Trevor?" Adam said and picked up a whistle.

When he blew it Christopher froze in place, a blank expression on his face.

"Now Mr. Trevor, come over here," Adam ordered and the author obeyed the command.

"Now, who am I?" Adam asked.

"You are Adam, AKA the Tickle Meister," Christopher replied.

"Alright, now your dream is about to come true," Adam said and by this time Timmy was fully awake, and also wondering what in all hell was going on. He saw his fellow officer, Jonathan Carlson still out cold, wearing nothing but his uniform trousers…and now his good buddy Christopher Trevor seemed to be under the Tickle Meister's control.

"Remove Timmy's shoes," Adam ordered Christopher and the author did just that.

"Hey, wait a second there, you don't want to do that," Timmy blurted.

"Oh yes he does, believe me, he truly does want to do that," Adam replied.

Timmy narrowed his eyes and decided to see where this would go. He then watched as Christopher removed his shoe and sniffed the inside of it. Timmy nearly groaned at the sight of that. Off came his other shoe as Christopher did the same thing with it. Timmy melted and finally let out the groan he had been bighting back. Adam and Christopher were pleased.

"Now sniff his toes," Adam commanded and Christopher again did as he was told.

"MMMMMMM…" Christopher crooned.

Adam saw that his buddy was enjoying this.

"Now lick his sole," Adam said.

"Oh man," Timmy reacted as his blue eyes rolled in his head.

Adam chuckled as Christopher started sucking on Timmy's socked toes. It was obvious that Timmy was in heaven and said, "Oh Christopher!! That feels so fucking good!!"

With that Adam sat back and watched as his friend did what he did best, namely servicing men's feet… But this had been a fantasy of Christopher's for so long now that Adam was happy to have helped to make his buddy's dream a reality…

As Officer Jonathan Carlson again began to come to Adam quickly dosed him again with more knockout gas from his walking stick…

"I'll get to you later my handsome friend," Adam said and sat back to enjoy the show…

ABOUT THE AUTHOR

Christopher Trevor was born in July 1963 and grew up in New York City. As soon as he was old enough to know how he began writing fiction and has been writing gay erotic/fetish stories for the past ten to twelve years at this point. He became an avid reader as well from the time he knew how and reads everything from fiction, to non-fiction to biographies of interesting and unusual people, people who have made a difference or who have paved the way for others. Christopher attributes his writing artistic inspiration to artists such as Etienne, Tom of Finland, Tagame, The Hun, and most notably Joe T, who Christopher

has had the pleasure of speaking with and even meeting over the last few years. Christopher states, "Joe T encouraged me to write about my fetish because I was embarrassed about it at the time. Joe T said that when we are embarrassed about something that makes it even more enticing somehow." Christopher totally agreed and never stopped writing in this genre. Erotic writers who inspired Christopher Trevor were: Tom Shaw (author of "That

Day at the Quarry), C.S. White (author of Big Sur), Larry Townsend (author of countless erotic novels), and Mason Powell (author of the classic story "The Brig.")

Christopher discovered that not only did he enjoy writing erotic tales but that after his first bondage experience he had a genuine flair for it. Writing to erotic oriented magazines about his first bondage experience truly opened the floodgates for Christopher where this style of writing is concerned. Christopher thanks the handsome and muscular "Greg" for that experience way back in time. Christopher took "Creative Writing" courses every semester during his high school years and while other friends of his stopped writing what they loved to write about as time went on Christopher never let a day go by when he didn't write something... "I feel that if I don't write every day I will die," Christopher has said many times over.

Foot fetish stories and all things related; spanking fetish, erotic shaving, muscle bondage, tickle torture, and hardcore stories are just a few of the areas of gay eroticism that Christopher enjoys writing about and inspiring in others as well. As one internet buddy said to Christopher where the black socks fetish is concerned, "Until I started talking with you I never gave a thought to my socks when I got dressed for work in the morning. Now when I pull my dress socks on every morning I get a chill up my spine."

Christopher is proud of the erotic effect he has on people...

Christopher Trevor is also the author of:

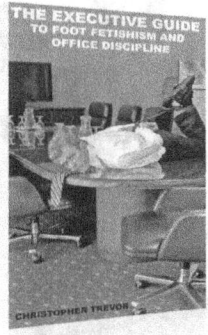

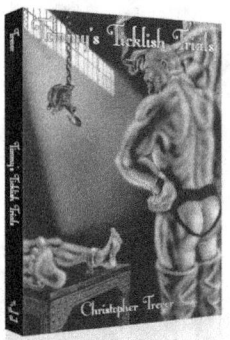

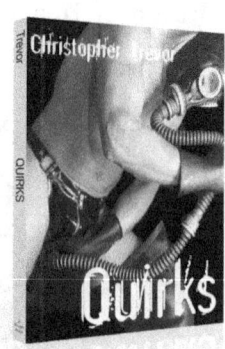

**Look for them where you bought this book,
Amazon.com or TheNazcaPlainsCorp.com.**

www.ingramcontent.com/pod-product-compliance
Lightning Source LLC
Chambersburg PA
CBHW051148260626
47170CB00005B/2005